PENGUIN ⟨Ⓟ⟩ CLASSICS

OROONOKO

Little is known about APHRA BEHN'S early life, from what religious and social background she came or how she obtained her extraordinary education, which allowed her to translate from French with ease, to allude frequently to the classics and to take part in the philosophical, political and scientific debates of her time. She was probably born around 1640 in Kent and in the early 1660s claims to have visited the British colony of Surinam, which forms the setting of her best-known short story, *Oroonoko, or the History of the Royal Slave* (1688), an early discussion of slavery and innate nobility. In 1666 she was employed by Charles II's government as a spy in Antwerp during the Dutch wars; inadequately paid, she turned to literature for a living, writing poetry, political propaganda for the Tory party and numerous short stories, as well as adapting or composing at least nineteen stage plays, many of them extremely successful, such as the comic depiction of Cavalier exile, *The Rover* (1677), and an early farce, *The Emperor of the Moon* (1687). During the political upheavals of the end of Charles II's reign and the beginning of James II's she wrote her great amorous and political novel, *Love-Letters between a Nobleman and His Sister*, which both satirizes and comments on the turbulent times. She had strong sympathy for Roman Catholicism but was also drawn to the sceptical and materialist philosophy of the libertines with whom she associated. Virginia Woolf acclaimed her as the first English woman to earn her living by writing, declaring, 'All women together ought to let flowers fall upon the tomb of Aphra Behn, for it was she who earned them the right to speak their minds.'

JANET TODD is the Francis Hutcheson Professor of English Literature at the University of Glasgow and an Honorary Fellow of Lucy Cavendish College, Cambridge. Her publications include *Women's Friendship in Literature* (1980), *Feminist Literary History* (1988), *The Sign of Angellica: Women, Writing and Fiction 1660–1800* and three biographies, *The Secret Life of Aphra Behn*

(1996), *Mary Wollstonecraft: A Revolutionary Life* (2000) and *Rebel Daughters: Rebellion in Ireland 1798* (2003). She has edited *Collected Letters of Mary Wollstonecraft* (Penguin, 2003) and is the general editor of the Cambridge edition of Jane Austen's works.

APHRA BEHN

Oroonoko

Edited with an Introduction and Notes by
JANET TODD

PENGUIN BOOKS ·

PENGUIN BOOKS

Published by the Penguin Group
Penguin Books Ltd, 80 Strand, London WC2R ORL, England
Penguin Putnam Inc., 375 Hudson Street, New York, New York 10014, USA
Penguin Books Australia Ltd, 250 Camberwell Road, Camberwell, Victoria 3124, Australia
Penguin Books Canada Ltd, 10 Alcorn Avenue, Toronto, Ontario, Canada M4V 3B2
Penguin Books India (P) Ltd, 11 Community Centre, Panchsheel Park, New Delhi – 110 017, India
Penguin Books (NZ) Ltd, Cnr Rosedale and Airborne Roads, Albany, Auckland, New Zealand
Penguin Books (South Africa) (Pty) Ltd, 24 Sturdee Avenue, Rosebank 2196, South Africa

Penguin Books Ltd, Registered Offices: 80 Strand, London WC2R ORL, England

www.penguin.com

First published by William Canning in 1688
Penguin Classics edition first published in 2003
023

Set in 10.25/12.25 pt PostScript Adobe Sabon
Typeset by Rowland Phototypesetting Ltd, Bury St Edmunds, Suffolk
Printed in England by Clays Ltd, St Ives plc

ISBN-13: 978–0–140–43988–5
ISBN-10: 0–140–43988–9

www.greenpenguin.co.uk

Contents

Acknowledgements

I owe a debt to previous excellent editors of *Oroonoko*, especially Catherine Gallagher and Joanna Lipking, and I have benefited from the work of the many scholars listed in the Further Reading. In addition I am grateful to Mary Ann O'Donnell for her generous sharing of her cataloguing of Behn studies and I have much appreciated the help of Derek Hughes, Jessica Munns, Bernard Dhuicq and Antje Blank. I should like to thank the British Academy for a small grant to aid in the preparation of the text.

Chronology

1640? Aphra Johnson probably born in Canterbury, Kent, the daughter of a barber or innkeeper, Bartholomew Johnson, and his wife Elizabeth.

1642 Outbreak of the Civil War and closing of the theatres.

1649 Charles I beheaded.

1651 Charles II with mainly Scottish troops defeated by Cromwell at the Battle of Worcester; Charles escaped and, en route to the Continent, hid in oak tree.

Lord Willoughby established a colony in Surinam; encouraged settlers, imported slaves.

1653 Oliver Cromwell became Lord Protector (died 1658).

1660 Charles II restored to the throne. He founded two theatre companies.

1663/4 Behn probably visited Willoughby's colony and encountered William Scot, son of a regicide.

Probably began her play *The Young King*.

*c.***1664** Probably married a London merchant of German extraction; he died or disappeared soon after. By 1666 was signing her name 'A. Behn'.

December: outbreak of the Great Plague in London.

1664 John Dryden and Sir Robert Howard's *The Indian Queen* produced.

1664–7 Second Dutch War between England and Holland.

1666 *July*: sent to Antwerp to obtain information about the Dutch from Scot. In debt by late 1666; Scot in a Dutch prison.

2 September: start of the Great Fire of London.

1667 Returned to England, heavily in debt, and may briefly have been imprisoned.

John Milton published *Paradise Lost*.

1670 First play, *The Forc'd Marriage*, staged by the Duke's Company; published the following year.

1671 *The Amorous Prince* performed and published; published poem to a fellow-playwright Edward Howard.

1672 Probably published *Covent Garden Drolery*, a collection of theatrical material, including several poems.

Royal African Company established. Over the next years it shipped thousands of slaves to Barbados in particular.

1673 *The Dutch Lover*, third performed play, published with an angry preface complaining she had been attacked because she was a woman.

1674–5 May have been kept by a lover John Hoyle, a bisexual lawyer, who seems to have been important to her over several years.

1676 Only tragedy, *Abdelazer*, performed, based on an earlier play; published the following year. *The Town-Fopp*, also based on an earlier play, performed.

1677 Another adaptation, *The Debauchee*, performed. Then *The Rover*, her most successful play, based on Thomas Killigrew's *Thomaso, or the Wanderer* (1664); published anonymously at first, later under her name.

1678 *Sir Patient Fancy*, one of her bawdiest plays, performed; published with a preface answering charges of plagiarism and bawdiness.

Popish Plot, a largely imaginary plot in which Roman Catholics were to oust Charles II.

1679 *The Feign'd Curtizans* performed with a prologue making clear her court sympathies; dedicated to Nell Gwyn, Charles II's mistress. *The Young King* possibly produced.

1680 Dryden published her poem 'A Paraphrase on Oenone to Paris' in his *Ovid's Epistles*.

The Revenge, another adaptation, performed. *The Second Part of the Rover* performed with politically committed prologue; published the following year.

Death of the poet the Earl of Rochester, for whom she wrote an elegy.

1681 *Song. To a New Scotch Tune* published, part of the government's propaganda against the Whigs. *The False Count* performed; published the following year. Behn was described as disputing for 'the Royal Cause'. Adaptation *The Roundheads*, her most extreme Tory play, performed; published the following year.

1681–2 Exclusion Crisis: Parliament Whigs tried to exclude Roman Catholic James from the throne. Charles II opposed them. The crisis brought about the creation of the first political parties, Whigs and Tories.

1682 *The City-Heiress* performed, again including a satire on Whigs.

Wrote poem to the aristocratic poet Anne Wharton, who had praised her Rochester elegy. Published prologue to *Like Father, Like Son*, a lost play, and prologue and epilogue to *Romulus and Hersilia*; the epilogue to the latter referred ungraciously to Charles II's illegitimate son, the Duke of Monmouth, and notices for the arrest of Behn and the actress speaking the lines were issued. If they were incarcerated, they seem to have been speedily freed.

Merging of the two dramatic companies, renamed the United Company; fewer new plays now required.

1683 *The Young King* published. 'To the Unknown Daphnis' published: a poem in praise of Thomas Creech's translation of Lucretius, which, in a later printed version, declared her religious scepticism.

June: Rye-House Plot to assassinate Charles II and his brother James discovered.

1684 Prologue written to Rochester's *Valentinian*. First part of *Love-Letters between a Nobleman and His Sister* published anonymously. *Poems upon Several Occasions* published: her only single-authored collection of poems, it included her long adaptation from the French, *Voyage to the Island of Love*.

1685 *6 February*: Death of Charles II and accession of James II. Failed rebellion of Monmouth, whom many Protestants wished to see as king in place of the Catholic James.

Wrote *Pindarick on the Death of Charles II*, *Poem to Catherine Queen Dowager* and *A Pindarick on the Happy Coronation of . . . James II*. Anonymously published second part of *Love-Letters*. Under own name published a poem in praise of Thomas Tryon's *The Way to Health, Long Life, and Happiness*; a collection of poems by several hands including her own, called *Miscellany*, together with a translation of La Rochefoucauld's maxims entitled *Seneca Unmasqued*.

Appealed to the United Company treasurer for an advance on her next play.

1686 Play *The Luckey Chance* performed.

Possibly helped compile the manuscript 'Astrea's Booke for Songs and Satyr's', a collection of satires now in the Bodleian Library, Oxford; published another French adaptation, *La Montre: or the Lover's Watch*.

1687 The pantomimic *The Emperor of the Moon* performed.

The Luckey Chance published with a rousing address to the reader, defending herself against the charge of bawdiness and declaring herself worthy of fame: 'All I ask, is the Priviledge for my Masculine Part the Poet in me . . .'; published her panegyric *To the Most Illustrious Prince Christopher Duke of Albemarle*, and the third part of *Love-Letters*, in which she described the downfall of Monmouth in the character of Cesario; published puffs for Sir Francis Fane's play *The Sacrifice* and Henry Higden's translation of Juvenal's tenth satire. Provided verses for a printing of *Aesop's Fables*. References to Behn's increasing ill health in her work and in satires on her.

1688 Published *Lycidus: or the Lover in Fashion* [second part of *Island of Love*] . . . *Together with a Miscellany of New Poems By Several Hands*. Translated two popular books by the French philosopher Fontenelle: *A Discovery of New Worlds* and *The History of Oracles*.

In response to Mary of Modena's pregnancy, wrote *A Congratulatory Poem . . . On the Universal Hopes . . . for a Prince of Wales*, followed after the birth by *Congratulatory Poem . . . On the Happy Birth of the Prince of Wales*. Published *Oroonoko*, *The Fair Jilt* and the translation *Agnes de Castro*. Poem to Sir Roger L'Estrange reasserted loyalty to James II, as did a criticism of another court poet in her satire *To Poet Bavius*. Wrote an elegy on the death of the poet Edmund

Waller. Published *Three Histories: Oroonoko, The Fair Jilt, Agnes de Castro*.

1 June: James imprisoned Anglican bishops for refusing to read his declaration of toleration in churches; they saw it as an attack on Protestantism.

10 June: James's son born.

29 June: trial of bishops began; they were acquitted with much popular jubilation. About this time invitation by several peers to William to invade was drafted.

July–August: William prepared for invasion, while James made political concessions, e.g. announcing intention to call a parliament.

28 September: William told States General of Holland of intended invasion, based on the invitation from James's subjects who wished to be saved from popery and slavery. Claimed he was invading to secure a free parliament not to dethrone James.

5 November: William landed at Torbay. Many English defected to his army.

9 December: Mary of Modena and the baby left for France.

11 December: James fled from London, was captured, but William gave orders he should be allowed to proceed to France, where he joined the queen and their son.

End December: William was de facto king.

1689 In *A Pindaric Poem to the Reverend Doctor Burnet* Behn refused an apparent request to praise William of Orange. Published 'Of Trees', a long verse translation of part of Abraham Cowley's Latin poem *Six Books of Plants* (1668). Greeted new queen Mary with *A Congratulatory Poem to Queen Mary*, in which she called the deposed James 'Great Lord, of all my Vows'.

13 February: Parliament offered crown to William and Mary, considering that James had abdicated.

11 April: William and Mary crowned in Westminster Abbey.

16 April: Aphra Behn died; buried in Westminster Abbey.

1689 *The Widdow Ranter* produced posthumously; published the following year. *The History of the Nun* and *The Lucky Mistake* published.

1696 *The Younger Brother, Or, The Amorous Jilt* performed and published with emendations. Thomas Southerne's adaptation of *Oroonoko* performed. The *Histories and Novels* published, including *La Montre* and the story 'Love-Letters'.

1698 *All the Histories and Novels* published, adding more stories: 'Memoirs of the Court of the King of Bantam', 'The Nun or the Perjured Beauty' and 'The Adventure of the Black Lady'.

1700 *Histories, Novels, and Translations* published, adding 'The Unfortunate Bride or the Blind Lady', 'The Dumb Virgin', 'The Unfortunate Happy Lady', 'The Wandring Beauty' and 'The Unhappy Mistake'.

Introduction

As a famous woman author Aphra Behn was unique in the Restoration, the period after 1660 when Charles II was restored to the English throne. She sustained a career through twenty eventful years. Hugely successful on the stage, she was also renowned for her erotic poetry and political propaganda on behalf of Charles II and his brother James II. By the time she turned to prose at the end of her life in the 1680s, she had a keen sense of her abilities. In the preface to a play staged in 1686 she wrote, 'I value Fame as much as if I had been born a *Hero*',[1] while *Oroonoko* ends with the boast, 'I hope the reputation of my pen is considerable enough to make his glorious name to survive to all ages'. After comparing painting and writing in her dedication to one of James II's ministers, Lord Maitland, she exulted that 'the pictures of the pen shall outlast those of the pencil, and even worlds themselves'. The exaggeration indicates how far she had come since the beginning of her career when she had seen herself simply as the author of entertaining plays. In a translation published in the year of her death, she inserted the plea, 'give my Verses Immortality'.[2] She would have relished the fame that *Oroonoko* has brought her in the twentieth century and the present day.

Aphra Behn and fiction

Aphra Behn had already been remarkable as the only female dramatist through most of the Restoration when she became a major writer of prose. Inevitably there are echoes in her stories of earlier fiction, of Elizabethan narratives, of French novellas, heroic romances and Spanish tales, but, except for one straight translation, no work of hers has a precise source. *Oroonoko* has no close parallel and no one in the seventeenth century wrote a story quite like it.

From 1670, through most of the reign of Charles II, Aphra Behn provided modish comedies for the stage. But towards the end of Charles's reign, the theatres were emptied by political plots as people began to fear the accession of his Catholic brother James. The two companies, The King's and the Duke's, which had been started just after the Restoration, had to merge and far fewer new plays were required. As a result, many dramatists moaned with Behn that 'a body has no creditt at the Playhouse as we used to have'.[3] At this point, the educated playwright turned to translation from the classics, as did England's poet laureate, John Dryden; Behn made some indifferent French poetry into more stylish English verse – then she moved into prose.

So Behn's preparation of five stories towards the end of her life can be partly explained by a need for money.[4] She revealed her poverty in a begging letter to her publisher, Jacob Tonson, in 1683, and in her negotiations in August 1685 with the deputy treasurer of the theatre company for which she wrote. Despite her laments, however, she was one of the few playwrights to have new and successful plays performed during the short reign of James II. She may not have been as poor by 1688 when she published her stories as she had been in the earlier part of the decade.

Beyond need of money Behn probably turned to prose because she enjoyed it. With it she could play with authorial control and investigate themes of love and obsession impossible in drama, which displayed the cut and thrust of sexual relations but not the inner life of a character or a changing personality through trying times. Fiction could do this, as she discovered with her first attempt, *Love-Letters between a Nobleman and His Sister*, a long novel based on fact and written over the politically tempestuous years of 1684–7 when James II came to the throne and began to lose it. The book followed the scandalous events in an aristocratic family and chronicled the failed rebellion of

Charles II's illegitimate son, the Duke of Monmouth, which darkened the first year of his uncle's reign. Anonymously published, the novel was a remarkable production, moving from heady epistolary form into cooler narrated fiction, and it gave Behn confidence in her powers as a storyteller.

One area of experimentation in *Love-Letters* and the short stories that followed is the narrator, sometimes female, sometimes of indeterminate sex. These narrators are not omniscient like those of nineteenth-century fiction but function as characters within the text. They place the action morally or satirically, validate events, stand for wavering public opinion and take the spotlight from the main character, who becomes less knowable and more ambiguous. The narrator of *Oroonoko* often identifies with her hero but also includes herself in the 'we' of the Europeans, so sharing their fear of Oroonoko's possible cruelty when baited, and she sometimes supports, sometimes controls him. She is boastful of her power at one time, at another clearly impotent. Thomas Southerne, who successfully dramatized Behn's story (in 1696) shortly after her death, wondered why such a great playwright had not written a play for her hero instead of 'burying' him in a novel. He speculated that she could not bear an actor to represent him or thought none could do it well. But the reason may have been generic: that the story was best told through the eyes of a narrator, with all the cultural complexity the device allowed, as well as the subtle interplay of a tale with its unstable, perhaps even at times duplicitous, teller. In a poem she wrote to a follower of William of Orange just after the fall of James II, Behn admitted that the victor controls history,[5] but *Oroonoko* suggests that a clever storyteller can evade this control.

Southerne made *Oroonoko* into heroic stage tragedy, a form Behn used only once: in another work about a black man, this one a villainous Moor called Abdelazer. Mostly she pulled away from the form, which usually required clear masculine heroism and moral absolutes. Yet at the end of her life she grew fascinated with the tragic mode in fiction; where only *Abdelazer* among her plays ends in death, three of the five stories end so, and another has a near death. Of these *Oroonoko* is the most

classically tragic, with its central character reminiscent of heroic
tragedy in his nobility, political significance, honour and truth.
Even here however the effect of the tragedy is not simply cathar-
tic. At the end the reader is in the position not of the spectator
at the close of a Shakespearian play or of the involved reader
of a realist novel, but rather of a person in the crowd at an
execution. The event of Oroonoko's death *is* tragic – there
was nothing more so, either in the Restoration or in the two
thousands years of Western art before it, than a prince or king
made impotent – but the actual details are grotesque. Southerne
ended his play more traditionally with Imoinda (a white woman
in his version) committing suicide and Oroonoko tidily dis-
patching both the governor and himself. Behn concludes with a
stinking corpse and a mangled body. With her narrative she had
already gained a strangeness beyond drama when her theatrical
noble hero suddenly became an ordinary man who might have
cut 'all our throats' (p. 68). The deaths go further and both
shock and appal with their unnerving physical detail.

Aphra Behn's life

The first (contemporary) biography makes Aphra Behn the
daughter of an intended lieutenant-general of Surinam and the
Caribbean islands, but these details are mainly taken from
Oroonoko, in which Behn cast herself as the narrator. In fact
she is more likely to have been born of humble parents in Kent,
with probably a barber for a father. The great unanswered
question of her childhood is, therefore, where she acquired the
extraordinary education which allowed her from her earliest
works to display a knowledge of European culture and to play
expertly with literary genres. What is certain is that she came to
loathe the Puritans who ruled England during the interregnum
between the execution of Charles I and restoration of his son
Charles II in 1660; she associated them with dishonour, joyless-
ness, commercial values and the controlling of women.

According to Colonel Thomas Colepeper, a relative of the
aristocratic Sidneys, Aphra's mother was his wet-nurse and it
may have been through him that she spied for royalists in the

Low Countries before the Restoration and then for Charles II's government in Surinam. There, according to reports, someone nicknamed 'Astrea' after a character in a French romance was associating with the undesirable parliamentarian William Scot, nicknamed 'Celadon' after the romance lover of Astrea. (Later Behn used the name 'Astrea' in her literary works as her *nom de plume*). When Astrea left Surinam, Celadon followed. In London Aphra apparently married a merchant of German extraction living there, possibly the Johann Behn who had served on a ship in the Caribbean. Whoever he was, she immediately lost him through death – or more likely separation since she never called herself a widow. Then in 1666, the year of the Great Fire of London, 'A. Behn', code-named 'Astrea', was dispatched as a royalist agent to Antwerp where she once more liaised with William Scot; England was at war with the Dutch, and Scot, in Dutch pay, was offering Dutch secrets to the English.[6]

As a spy Behn was not a complete success. She was fooled by Scot, who was acting as a triple agent, while a rival spy claimed she was too garrulous and open. After some months her English masters stopped paying her. As a result she returned to England penniless and was threatened with debtors' prison. At this point she turned to the stage. She claimed she had already written a play in Surinam but her début occurred with *The Forc'd Marriage*, which opened the 1670 season of one of the two theatre companies. The prologue wittily alluded to her sex and past: 'The Poetess too, they say, has Spies abroad.' There followed at least eighteen more plays, making Behn the most prolific dramatist of the period between 1670 and 1690. Some such as *The Rover* were extremely popular and associated her with the kind of comedy that displayed witty couples, spirited women and rakish men, very much the types of people who frequented Charles II's court. Behn was an admirer of the major royal mistresses and her first dramatic dedication was to Nell Gwyn. To support the court and its flamboyant ethos, Behn also turned to writing politically engaged plays when the royal government came under attack from those she regarded as heirs of the old Puritans.

Behn was also a successful poet, gaining fame for her erotic but never crude poems of female passion. Although she was satirized for promiscuity, her name was consistently associated only with one man, John Hoyle, a bisexual lawyer with a reputation for violence, republicanism and freethinking. Her darkening depictions of libertines in her plays may have drawn on Hoyle, as may her most complex love poems, which describe the painful ambiguities of physical and ideal love. At the same time Behn seems to have responded to many other people, and her works, which may or may not have an autobiographical component, address both men and women amorously. She appreciated beauty where she found it.

In the 1680s, very unusually for a woman, Behn was associated with freethinking, as is suggested in a poem she wrote for a young man, Thomas Creech, who had just translated a philosophical work by the Latin poet Lucretius.[7] The translator was aware of his dangerously unchristian subject-matter and tried to defang it, but Behn saw the work as a triumphant assertion of rationalism and materialism, a victory of reason over faith. She also wrote a curious paraphrase on the Lord's Prayer in which she moaned that authors could not earn their 'daily Bread' and declared 'Trespasses' were not to be resisted.

By 1688 she was both personally and politically anxious. She knew she was dying and she felt the crumbling of the royal regime of the Stuarts which she had so strenuously supported. She feared that, if James II fell, the country would return both to the restrictive morality of the Puritans and to the political anarchy of the Civil War which had been raging when she was a child. In fact she lived just long enough to see the remarkably peaceful ousting of James and the arrival of his nephew and daughter as the joint sovereigns William and Mary. It was not a change she relished but she had little time to adjust since she died a few days after their coronation in 1689.

In her last years she seems to have been remembering her youth: the first three of her stories as well as her final play *The Widdow Ranter* all draw on material from this time. Her months in Surinam and Antwerp had been important for her development as a writer. In Surinam she had allegedly begun her first play and, if the unknown author of 'The History of the Life and Memoirs of Mrs. Behn' (1698) is to be believed, in Antwerp, when her services as a spy were no longer needed, she began writing amusing prose. The city later provided the setting for *The Fair Jilt*, based on a real trial and botched execution (Behn was fascinated by executions, often rather carnivalesque public events during her lifetime, and she used them as the climax of several of her novels). Surinam gave the background for *Oroonoko*, which tells of men known to have been active there in the 1660s and describes the sort of events that pepper private reports and state records. Her portrayal of the colony as paradisaical in its natural resources but hellish in its human arrivals was supported by the Baptist pamphleteer Henry Adis who was deeply shocked by the brutish nature of the Surinam settlers. To him they displayed debauchery and atheism and were even worse than 'the very Heathens themselves, to the shame and stink of Christianity'. Collectively, the Europeans were a 'rude rabble', given to drunkenness, blasphemous oaths and 'lascivious Abominations'.[8]

Slavery and colonization

Surinam was a difficult region to settle and control. On his third expedition to the New World in 1498, Columbus had arrived at the mouth of the Orinoco (or Oroonoko as it was often spelt) on the north coast of South America. He believed he had reached the river which led to the Earthly Paradise. The region of Surinam was not truly conquered by the Spanish or Portuguese in the sixteenth and seventeenth centuries and so was a target for colonial activity by many later exploring nations, especially the French, Dutch and English.

In 1647 Lord Willoughby received from the English government a twenty-one-year lease of property rights in the Caribee islands. He became governor of Barbados and aimed at founding a new colony in Surinam. In 1651 a party of about three hundred was sent out from Barbados – the fourteenth attempt at settlement.[9] Plantations were begun along the Surinam River and soon there were about five hundred in all. Although the overwhelming motive of all the settlers was financial, factional politics inevitably travelled with them, and Behn's presence there may well have attested to the sense in England that political rebels might use the colonies for their own ends and even negotiate with England's enemies, especially the Dutch. Presiding over the mixture of greed and grumbling, of renegades, adventurers, political exiles, indentured labourers, felons and property-starved younger sons that made up the colony was Lord Willoughby's old political associate William Byam, now made his deputy governor.[10] By the 1660s the colony's purpose was largely to produce sugar for the English market; since sugar was an expensive crop, the planters tended to have large estates demanding copious labour.

Most visitors saw the Native Americans or Indians of the region either as happy innocents to be taught Christianity and culture or as cannibalistic savages to be suppressed. Some had mixed feelings, such as the writer George Warren, who found them cowardly and treacherous, but also hoped they might be christianized. According to the Dutch traveller Esquemelin, before the European invasion of the region they were barbarous, sensual, brutish and idle, rousing themselves only to fight each other. It was generally agreed by European observers that the climate made them lazy and that they lacked northern shame. Behn, however, saw them through the lens of romance. In her pages they inhabited a pastoral Arcadia or a Golden Age of innocence when words were 'simple' and souls 'sincere'. Her predecessor here is the sixteenth-century French essayist Montaigne, who wrote in a tolerant essay about 'cannibals' on this coast (which he had never visited) that they were close to nature and had no 'words that signifie Lying, Treachery, Dissimulation, Avarice, Envy, Detraction and Pardon'.[11] A more contemporary voice using the Golden Age myth was that of John Milton, who in *Paradise Lost* called God 'the sov'reign Planter' and contrasted a pastoral world associated with Adam and Eve with a greedy commercialization promoted by Satan, the profit-driven 'great adventurer'.[12] Like Surinam and a fading Golden Age realm, the earth became a colonial outpost, a receptacle of contending outcasts.

Despite accepting the romantic image of Surinam, Behn had no problem with England's imperial adventures in the Americas – unlike many of her compatriots who dismissed this overseas activity not as culturally inappropriate but as expensive and destabilizing for England. For Behn, the New World could seem both prelapsarian and a rich commercial opportunity. In *The Widdow Ranter*, written about the same time as *Oroonoko* and the first play ever to be set in an English colony, she made her hero – a figure very like Oroonoko – aware of the injustice in conquest but also believe that the conqueror had the right to maintain what he had won by skill or force. In *Oroonoko* she lamented that Charles II had not seen the potential of his colony and that, shortly after she left, he had let it go – in exchange for New Amsterdam, later renamed New York.

To develop Surinam through labour, Willoughby had urged settlers to come from Britain. But the colonies had difficulty attracting bona fide immigrants and most suspected that advertisements and favourable reports lied about conditions. The colonies imported indentured labour from Britain, especially from the outlying regions of Ireland, Scotland and Wales, and accepted political prisoners more or less exiled and enslaved for life, but there were never enough. Until this point the African slave-trade, established long before by the Portuguese and Spanish to feed Mediterranean needs and later their new colonies in South America, had not been much exploited by the English, who had no slavery at home or much sense of chattel slavery (where people could be bought and sold and their children automatically enslaved); when they went to Africa, they were most interested in gold. In 1630, however, they officially entered the trade when Charles I granted the first licence for slave-transporting. By 1672, a Royal African Company had been established for slaving; it spent much time fending off the new slaving power, the Dutch, as well as negotiating with the African sellers who played off one European nation against another to get the best prices. Unlike the relationship with the Americas, where the Europeans came to settle in spite of the natives (who by the time the English arrived had long suffered harrying from Spanish and Portuguese), that with Africa was strictly commercial, and forts were established along the coast only for trade, carried on by permission of the slave-selling African chiefs. Among the trading posts founded by the English on the Gold Coast (modern Ghana) was the one mentioned as Coramantien in *Oroonoko*, variously controlled in the 1660s by the English and Dutch. The imperial adventures were in their infancy and Behn did not assume in her audience knowledge of South American colonies, of their friendly inhabitants or of African slavery.

Behn's Africa is the first fictional depiction by an English writer of African life below the Sahara. Yet, where her account of Surinam has the ring of eye-witness truth, the Africa she portrayed has little in common with the West Africa described by French and English travellers and traders. Depictions of the old customs of the Fantis and Ashantis in the Gold Coast are not especially connected to the oriental activities and harem intrigues of Behn's fantastic kingdom; the matrilineal, polygamous societies of West Africa have little to do with patrilineal kingship and the undying love between the monogamous Oroonoko and Imoinda. In fact her hero fuses cultures. He is an African in the New World, with a European liberal education giving him not the usual Christianity but a scepticism with which he can judge the Christian Europeans. At the same time, like her other black creation, the villainous Abdelazer, Oroonoko is a non-European prince who recalls the Moorish or Turkish stereotype of a character in whom the common European urge to power is presumed to course without European checks, to the destruction of himself and those around him.

In the seventeenth century the English did not consider Africans as the only natural slaves. They themselves had white slaves in Barbados and treated many European indentured servants as virtual slaves. On ships and in colonies Catholics felt it reasonable to enslave Protestants and vice versa. Although the physical beauty of the 'gloomy race' (p. 13) was rarely stressed, blackness remained to some extent a glamorous concept: in the Restoration, *Othello* (1602-4) with its black hero was the favourite Shakespearian tragedy and Ben Jonson's *Masque of Blackness* (1605) had exotically displayed court ladies blackened into

'Ethiopians' – even though in the sequel they lost their blackness. In these depictions there is little of the sense of colour as a racial curse – the notion of Negroes as descended from Cain or Noah's accursed son Ham, doomed to be servants of servants – although it was already current in some quarters. Inevitably, however, the later history of prejudice is sometimes read back into these early works, as it is into *Oroonoko*.

At the time and for about a century afterwards, as illustrations to published versions of Southerne's play version reveal, the hero in *Oroonoko* was both exotic and culturally assimilated. In 1776 Mr Savigny played him in full court dress with the addition of a vestigial toga. Like other heroes he speaks with the rhetoric of ancient Roman nobility, and the civility and courtliness of both Oroonoko and Imoinda allow assumptions about class and gender to be transcultural. Oroonoko is a prince in all depictions, despite having no country to rule and no means of getting one either through his own efforts or through the help of those who, perhaps in part for their own entertainment, have accepted his royal status. Although often dismissed as racist, Behn's depiction of Oroonoko as unlike other Africans, with his Roman nose, straight hair and extreme blackness, can be read as a simple desire to make him distinct, other, the cynosure of all noble men.

Although in the 1660s, when *Oroonoko* was set, slavery was hugely increasing in the English Caribbean islands, it was not yet a large social issue in England and nothing approaching an abolitionist movement appeared until almost a century after Behn's time. Yet even then there were isolated voices of protest. One belonged to her eccentric, mystical and vegetarian acquaintance Thomas Tryon, who later wrote *Friendly Advice to the Gentleman-Planters of the East and West Indies* (1684). In one section, 'Discourse in way of Dialogue, between an *Ethiopean* or *Negro-Slave* and a *Christian*', he presents a noble African asking his master 'what makes us your *Slaves* . . . to be thus Lorded and Tyrannized over by you?' He continues: 'we are human *rational Souls*, and as much the *Image of God* as [your]-selves, and want none of the noble Faculties, therefore our *innocent Blood* will equally call for *Ve[n]geance*'. In another section, 'The Negro's Complaint of their Hard Servitude, and the Cruelties Practised upon them', he associates African slavery with European habits of luxury, commerce and cruelty: 'For though we are . . . made in thine Image, and endued with rational and immortal Souls, yet we are nothing more in many of our Masters esteem, than *their Money* and if some of them could find out a way to torment and plague us tenfold more, they would do it, provided we might still be but able to perform our Drudgery, to maintain them in Superfluity and Gluttony.'[13] Another protest came from Morgan Godwyn, a Protestant minister in Virginia and Barbados in the 1660s and 1670s, who wrote *The Negro's and Indian's Advocate* (1680). He did not challenge slavery but argued for the humanity of Africans, and he criticized their cruel treatment by West Indian planters. Since 'God had made (of one blood) all Nations of Men', he proposed converting the slaves to Christianity to promote their 'integrity and long-livedness'.[14] Conveniently this would also render them less prone to rebellion, a constant fear in these colonies where slaves rapidly came to outnumber their masters.

Like almost all her contemporaries, Aphra Behn accepted slavery for most of the enslaved; Oroonoko's first present to Imoinda is a group of slaves and he later bargains for his freedom by offering to send slaves to Surinam. But the enslaving of someone born noble was anathema to her and the later sense that a whole race could, without distinctions, be traded and treated quite unlike any other would have appalled her. Where for the colonists the crucial difference was between Christian and infidel, for Behn and other dramatists rank overtopped race and religion. Twenty years before she wrote, Dryden with his co-author Sir Robert Howard made the Aztecs honourable in his *Indian Queen* (1664), which Behn mentions in her work (p. 10). In all the exotic dramas of the time, nobles recognize each other across cultures. In Southerne's words in his *Oroonoko*, it is horrific to enslave a man of rank from any race who was 'born only to Command': 'here's a Prince . . . among the Slaves, and you set him down to go as a Common man,' protests one character.[15]

Although Behn did not have the modern concept of slavery,

then, she did have a sense of the improper commodification of human beings for money, against which she protests in many of her works, and indeed Oroonoko makes a distinction between enslaving battle-victims and slaving for money. Prostitutes and women sold into marriage are sympathetically treated, and in her 1686 play, *The Luckey Chance*, she condemned a husband for giving his wife's sexual favours as payment for a gambling debt. So too she sometimes lamented that an author had, for money, to betray art in order to please. The sense of commodification of bodies and talent is at its extreme in the slave-trade, and a contemporary protest about the pricing of slaves can exemplify an attitude which she never held: 'negroes cost a third to a half more than they did, and are difficult to procure ... many ships have been unable to procure negroes, and after lying many months have left with but half their load of negroes, though with cargo all dispersed. Also, we have often lost a half to a third of the negroes shipped ... Negroes are not only very chargeable and perishable, but it is impracticable to keep any quantity unsold for many days; we must part with them for what we can get.'[16]

Behn may have gone to an extreme, presenting a slave who never does a stroke of work, descends from a line of literary noble savages and candid infidels, and speaks in the high rhetoric of heroic tragedy, but yet, with all these literary devices, she managed to convey a sense of the horror of slavery itself which no other work of the time quite caught. While intellectually often accepting the state – slavery and colonialism – her generically unstable work allows both of them to be probed and considered: readers may read sometimes with her, sometimes from her subtext, and sometimes against the grain.

Political context of *Oroonoko*

Throughout her life Behn was a political writer, steeped in the controversies and day-to-day politics of her age. Her works are royalist, fiercely supporting the regimes of the Stuart brothers, Protestant Charles and the Catholic James. Perhaps she herself was a Catholic, but her writings, including *Oroonoko*, suggest

she had little religious belief of any sort, although she certainly
enjoyed the pageantry and ritual of Catholicism and understood
that religion formed part of the state's proper control. In her
Oroonoko dedication she clearly accepted Catholicism as one
of King James's attributes.

For Behn in her praise poems, James II was an heroic figure,
noble and guileless, a great leader of men. By 1688, however,
she could see his flaws even as she continued to hymn his
reign. So her works taken together give a divided message: the
panegyrics wholly supportive, the fictions admiring but also
admonitory. The king's simple, heroic personality was out of
kilter with the debased modern and complex world of England,
a world exaggerated in her depictions of Surinam in *Oroonoko*
and of Virginia in *The Widdow Ranter*. Both regions lacked a
high-born governor and, in the chaos into which they fell, noble
souls such as the slave Oroonoko and the rebel Bacon of *The
Widdow Ranter* became powerless. The point was stressed to
Behn's dedicatee, Lord Maitland: if such a nobleman as he had
been able to protect the slave prince in Surinam, the latter 'had
not made so Inglorious an end'.

Oroonoko is not transparently political like *Love-Letters* and
the praise poems; yet political parallels and references abound.
It was probably written in 1688 after the announcement of
Queen Mary's pregnancy, when the Catholic James II tottered
on his throne and rumours were rife of a great Armada being
assembled by the Dutch Protestant William, invited to rule
by disloyal English peers. It was printed just after her poem
celebrating the royal birth, in which the story was advertised
for sale. At this point Behn was one of the few poets to welcome
the continuation of the Stuart line and to have urged the need
for royal lineage and legitimacy to keep the peace. At the same
time she encoded James's predicament and her own perplexity
in works that presented heroes of wondrous firmness but little
life-saving flexibility. In *Oroonoko*, the death and defeat of a
naïve royal hero comes just as his child is about to be born – the
birth of a Prince of Wales would signal the end of James's reign
since for many it threatened a continuation of Catholic rule into
the future. Good people failed to save Charles I – admired by

Oroonoko – and this beheaded king must form some warning to his beleaguered son. James II was often called Caesar – as Oroonoko is – and the dark Stuarts were referred to as 'black'. Surinam, where Oroonoko is killed, fell to the ignoble and mercenary Dutch shortly afterwards: England itself was about to fall to the Dutch William.

The glamorous and glorious conception of personal power which Oroonoko and Bacon hold resembles that of heroic drama. They recall the mythologized 1640s, when cavaliering was swashbuckling, or the 1660s, when the myths were fashioned, the early jubilant years of the Restoration with their fantastic hopes of a Golden Age and incorruptible power. Oroonoko believes in a kind of transcendental politics, true for all times and places, a belief based on heroic myths and deeply embedded in masculine classical literature like Plutarch's *Lives*, which he most valued. He believes, with Bacon, in the integrity of language: the oath and word of honour. Renaissance tragedy, especially Shakespeare's, persistently expressed a belief that oratorical virtuosity could dominate the rudest rabble. The Restoration had abandoned the notion, but it remains dear to the heart of both Behn's vanquished heroes. Behn herself knew that it had little to do with *realpolitik*. Oroonoko's great speeches inspire his followers but do not sustain them.

Oroonoko, a richly evocative tale, is not straight political allegory of course, and the fictional character of the slave prince is not simply a substitute for James, but the story *is* surely being informed by the impending political tragedy of an historical man. If James and his followers failed to see the analogy immediately, Behn made it clearer in the dedication: 'men of eminent parts are as exemplary as even monarchs themselves, and virtue is a noble lesson to be learnt, and it is by comparison we can judge and choose.'

Criticism and Aphra Behn's reputation

Although in many places morally shocking, Behn's fiction was not as sexually risqué as her plays and it did not suffer the wholesale opprobrium accorded her drama from the late eighteenth century onwards. It simply fell out of print, except for *Oroonoko*, which took on a quite new cultural life. The history of this story's critical reception is the history of fashionable movements and causes.

The pre-eminence of *Oroonoko* would have surprised its author, who, although she admitted spending much time and effort on her long allegorical poem *Voyage to the Island of Love*, a work hardly mentioned by modern critics, had on her own admission dashed off *Oroonoko* in one sitting of a few hours in her last year of life. Also, since she was loud in complaints that men gained more fame than she did for similar work, she might wryly have noted that much of the renown of her story came through Southerne's stage version. In this the political history Behn had enshrined was largely evaded – inevitably so, since, between the writing and the acting, the tragic fall of James II had been reinterpreted and named the Glorious Revolution, a landmark on England's route to parliamentary democracy and constitutional monarchy. In England, in the eighteenth century, as Dutch gave way to German kings without any huge change to the national psyche and culture, the history Behn had mediated was largely forgotten. *Oroonoko* became primarily a love story. *A General Dictionary* (1734–41) declared that in the tale Behn had drawn the 'Passion of Love with great delicacy and softness'. However, it suggested that racial views had shifted since the Restoration, for it commented: 'A difference of colour does not make any difference in the soul ... tho' some nations of Blacks appear incorrigible brutes, there yet are others, who discover a natural fund of wit and genius.'[17]

With the Cult of Sensibility and the growth of humanitarian sentiment in the mid-eighteenth century, *Oroonoko* gained new currency. The slave-trade was at its height, slavery was a fully developed system, and the sense of its racial basis had increased. In this atmosphere a schizophrenic vision of Africans grew, very different from Behn's. Those who were benefiting financially from the slave-trade wept over the fall of an idealized African prince on the stage. When, in 1749, a real Fanti prince with the patina of Oroonoko appeared in London with his noble

companion and attended the play, the audience enjoyed being
further moved at the idea of these men witnessing Southerne's
representation. The prince gained great popularity when struck
'with that generous grief which pure nature always feels, and
which art had not yet taught them to suppress; the young prince
was so far overcome, that he was obliged to retire at the end of
the fourth act.'[18] By now some people were beginning to see
England less as a slaving nation than as the opponent of slavery,
and *Oroonoko* in its various theatrical transformations became
part of the mission to abolish the trade – in a 1760 version a
discussion was held with the overt intention of influencing the
audience against the slave-trade. In France *Oroonoko* gained
sentimental currency in 1745, shorn of its politics and gruesome,
mangling ending: in this version the happy multicultural and
multiracial pair set off back to Africa to be king and queen and
to send presents to their friend Aphra Behn. The French work
failed to enter the slavery debate, and in the 1769 edition
Oroonoko gives three hundred slaves to the captain who takes
him home.[19]

Curiously Behn's and Southerne's works played little part in
the British effort actually to stop the slave-trade at the end
of the eighteenth century, although the now mythical name
Oroonoko was invoked in poetic arguments about individual
suffering. In the nineteenth century, however, Behn's story
became part of the emancipation struggle to destroy slavery as
well as the trade. Considered to have superior moral authority,
women were always important in the movement, and an article
in the *Dublin University Magazine* of 1856 and a review in the
St James's Magazine of 1863 both compared Behn's *Oroonoko*
to Harriet Beecher Stowe's recently published *Uncle Tom's
Cabin*. This approach allowed some critics to appreciate Aphra
Behn who would otherwise have been repulsed by her unfemi-
nine and libertine attitudes, as well as her royalist Tory politics.
So, for example, Julia Kavanagh in 1863 could berate her for
loving 'grossness for its own sake' and sinking her sex 'to the
level of man's coarseness',[20] yet redeem her for creating her
noble African prince. Ernest Baker, in his 1905 volume of Behn's
short novels, claimed that, although she manifested an awful

tendency to lewdness elsewhere, Behn had written the admirable *Oroonoko*, 'the first emancipation novel'.[21]

With the post-colonial interest in bodies and race in the 1980s *Oroonoko* became a favoured text.[22] A paradise of analysis was discovered in the work; its sometimes awkward changes in style became multiple discourses and its often noted contradictions turned into subversions of its dominant ideas. What had been eliminated in the eighteenth century became central: the blackness of Oroonoko and Imoinda, their mutilated bodies. *Oroonoko* destabilized many oppositions of gender and race and became a critique of colonialism and resistant to colonialist stereotypes; at the same time it illuminated both consciously and unconsciously European attitudes to African slavery.

The other literary critical context was feminist. This criticism brought attention to the figure of the narrator, both with her literary and representational power and with her political impotence at crucial moments. It also threw light on her relationship with the beautiful and murdered Imoinda, who is physically represented – she dances and stumbles, pulls the knife to her, and breeds a child – but who is largely kept voiceless while the narrator dominates with her words. Imoinda's child will not be born to give his father immortality; instead, that will come from the narrator's depiction. So the narrator has in a way won the hero from his wife, he and she are celebrities and superior tellers of truth. In this criticism, the traditionally submissive but physically fierce Imoinda seems to hold a strangeness not quite achieved by the heroic Oroonoko; she is decorative and exotic, 'japanned' (p. 48) like oriental carving, and it is her corpse that becomes a stinking object covered with flowers (p. 73), while the narrator remains very much alive.

Aphra Behn was a mistress of her craft, and the explosion of criticism on *Oroonoko* is not simply a symptom of our times, but also a part of a necessary rehabilitation of a writer with much to reveal about late seventeenth-century society and early women's lives, fantasies and constraints, as well as the relationship of the female pen to the wider patriarchal culture. Aphra Behn is crucial in the history of women's writing; she was a good dramatist and poet, but women's literary future lay primarily

in fiction, and her achievement in *Oroonoko* makes her an
important predecessor of a line of renowned female novelists.
Yet the story is more than an early example of fiction, distinctive
because written by a woman; with its significance for our understanding of early notions of race, colonialism, class and gender,
this mélange of courtly romance, heroic tragedy and New World
traveller's tale has become a disturbing, troubling classic, as
exotic as Oroonoko himself.

                                                     Janet Todd

NOTES

1. Prologue to *The Luckey Chance* (1687), in *The Works of Aphra
    Behn*, ed. Janet Todd, 7 vols. (London: W. Pickering, 1992–6),
    7.217.
2. 'Of Plants. Book VI' (1689), *Works* 1.325. Only quotations from
    Oroonoko have been modernized.
3. See my biography, *The Secret Life of Aphra Behn* (London: André
    Deutsch, 1996; Pandora, 1999), p. 325.
4. Of the fourteen tales ascribed to Behn five were published just
    before and after her death in 1689, all bearing her name:
    Oroonoko, The Fair Jilt, The History of the Nun, Agnes de Castro
    and *The Lucky Mistake*. They have an authenticity impossible
    for the later works published some years after her death. These
    may be by her and there are touches that indicate her authorship,
    but some may be forgeries since her prose legacy seems to have
    fallen into the hands of three young men, each unscrupulous in a
    different way: Thomas Brown, poet, satirist and literary forger;
    Charles Gildon, fictionist, translator and man of letters; and
    Samuel Briscoe, an eccentric bookseller. In the 1690s, all three
    pressingly needed money – indeed Briscoe went bankrupt during
    these years. A contemporary, John Dunton, remarked, 'by con-
    tracting a friendship with Tom Brown [Briscoe] will grow rich as
    fast as his author can write or hear from the Dead, so that honest
    Sam does, as it were, thrive by his misfortunes' (Brown wrote
    Letters from the Dead to the Living). Conceivably one of the
    'dead' from whom they heard was Aphra Behn, whom Briscoe
    began publishing in 1696, just when the successful dramatization
    of her *Oroonoko* by Thomas Southerne gave Behn's name
    renewed currency.

5. *A Pindaric Poem to the Reverend Doctor Burnet On the Honour he did me of Enquiring after me and my Muse*, Works 1.307–10.
6. I have pursued the speculation concerning Behn's activities before the Restoration, as well as other aspects of her life, in *The Secret Life of Aphra Behn*, pp. 36–66.
7. *Works* 1.25–9.
8. Henry Adis, *A Letter Sent from Syrranam, to His Excellency, the Lord Willoughby of Parham* (London, 1664), pp. 4–5.
9. See William Byam, *The Description of Guyana*, British Library Sloane MS 3662.
10. With the help of Byam, Willoughby had shifted from his initial support of Parliament and had tried to hold Barbados for the royal cause. He failed and, after his defeat, was restricted to his estates in Surinam. But he was eager to return to England, so after a short time he left Surinam to Byam. In England Willoughby was imprisoned and released only on condition that he return to Surinam. He was by now too deep into plotting and did not set out until well after the Restoration. Having backed the winning side, Willoughby was confirmed in a large portion of the proprietorship, now shared with Lord Clarendon's son, Laurence Hyde, under whom Byam continued as deputy governor.
11. *Essays of Michael Seigneur de Montaigne, rendered into English by Charles Cotton* (1685–6), 1.369. Behn probably read Montaigne between visiting Surinam and publishing *Oroonoko* in 1688, since Cotton, perhaps an acquaintance of hers, was translating the essays in the 1680s.
12. John Milton, *Paradise Lost*, IV.691 and X.440.
13. Thomas Tryon, *Friendly Advice to the Gentleman-Planters of the East and West Indies* (1684), pp. 162, 182, 188 and 109–10.
14. Morgan Godwyn, *The Negro's and Indians Advocate* (1680), pp. 18 and 147.
15. Thomas Southerne, *Oroonoko, a Tragedy* (1696), I.ii.42–3 and 173.
16. From the protest of the Royal African Company, 23 October 1683, *Cal. St. P. Col., 1681–1685*, pp. 525–6, quoted in Elizabeth Donnan, *Documents Illustrative of the History of the Slave Trade* (New York: Octagon, 1965), 1.317–18.
17. *A General Dictionary, Historical and Critical* (1735), 3.141.
18. *Gentleman's Magazine*, 19 February 1749, 89–90.
19. Pierre-Antoine de la Place, *Oronoko traduit de l'anglois* (Amsterdam, 1745). For a fuller discussion of the French translations, see

Jane Spencer, *Aphra Behn's Afterlife* (Oxford: Oxford University Press, 2000).

20. Julia Kavanagh, *English Women of Letters: Biographical Sketches* (1863), 1.21–2.

21. Ernest A. Baker, *The Novels of Mrs Aphra Behn* (1905), p. xxiii.

22. For a fuller discussion of critical fashions, see my *Critical Fortunes of Aphra Behn* (Columbia, SC: Camden House, 1998).

Further Reading

There are numerous modern editions of Behn's *Oroonoko*.
Two recent ones are the Bedford Cultural Edition by Catherine
Gallagher (Boston: Bedford/St Martin's, 2000) and the Norton
Critical Edition by Joanna Lipking (New York: W. W. Norton
& Co., 1997). Both provide a wealth of material on slavery and
the triangular trade of sugar and slaves.
Complete works: *The Works of Aphra Behn*, ed. Janet Todd,
7 vols. (London: William Pickering, and Ohio: Ohio State
University Press, 1992–6).

Adaptations of *Oroonoko*

Thomas Southerne, *Oroonoko, a Tragedy* (London, 1696).
Pierre-Antoine de la Place, *Oronoko traduit de l'anglois* [in two
    parts] (Amsterdam, 1745).
John Hawkesworth, *Oroonoko, a Tragedy* (London, 1759).
[Francis Gentleman], *Oroonoko: or, the Royal Slave. A tragedy.*
    Altered from Southerne (Glasgow, 1760).
Anon., *Oroonoko. A Tragedy. Altered from the Original Play*
    ... by the late Thomas Southerne (London, 1760).
John Ferriar, *The Prince of Angola, a Tragedy, altered from the*
    Play of Oroonoko (Manchester, 1788).
Biyi Bandele, *Aphra Behn's Oroonoko* [second half based on
    Hawkesworth's text] (Charlbury, Oxford, 1999).

Biographical studies

Duffy, Maureen, *The Passionate Shepherdess: Aphra Behn 1640–1689* (London: Cape, 1977).

Goreau, Angeline, *Reconstructing Aphra: A Social Biography of Aphra Behn* (New York: Dial, 1980).

Todd, Janet, *The Secret Life of Aphra Behn* (London: André Deutsch, 1996; Pandora, 1999).

Woodcock, G., *The Incomparable Aphra* (London: Boardman, 1948).

Historical background for Surinam

Biet, Antoine, *Voyage de la France équixonale en l'isle de Cayenne* (1654).

Dunn, Richard S., *Sugar and Slaves. The Rise of the Planter Class in the English West Indies 1624–1813* (Chapel Hill: University of North Carolina Press, 1972).

Ligon, Richard, *A True and Exact History of the Island of Barbados* (1657).

Ogilby, John, *America: Being the Latest, and Most Accurate Description of the New World* (London, 1671).

de Rochefort, Charles, *The History of the Caribby-Islands*, trans. John Davies of Kidwelly (1666).

Stedman, John Gabriel, *Narrative of a Five Years' Expedition, Against the Revolted Negroes of Surinam, in Guiana* (1796).

'Surinam Justice. In the Case Of several persons proscribed by certain Usurpers of Power in that Colony. Being a Publication of that perfect Relation of the beginning, Continuance, and End of the late Disturbances in the Colony of Surinam, set forth under that title, by William Byam Esq . . . and the Vindication of those Gentlemen, sufferers by his injustice, from the Calumnies wherewith he asperseth them in that Relation. Couched in the Answer thereunto by Robert Sanford' (London, 1662).

du Tertre, Jean-Baptiste, *Histoire Générale Des Antilles habitées par les François* (1677).

Tryon, Thomas, *Friendly Advice to the Gentlemen-Planters of the East and West Indies* (1684).

Warren, George, *Impartial Description of Surinam upon the Continent of Guiana in America* (1667).

Critical studies

Aravamudan, Srinivas, 'Petting Oroonoko', in *Tropicopolitans: Colonialism and Agency, 1688–1804* (Durham, NC: Duke University Press, 1999).

Ballaster, Ros, 'New hystericism: Aphra Behn's *Oroonoko*: The body, the text and the feminist critic', in *New Feminist Discourses: Critical Essays on Theories and Texts*, ed. Isobel Armstrong (New York: Routledge, 1992).

Brown, Laura, 'The romance of empire. *Oroonoko* and the trade in slaves', in *The New Eighteenth Century: Theory, Politics, English Literature*, ed. by Felicity Nussbaum and Laura Brown (New York: Methuen, 1987); reprinted in *The New Casebooks. Aphra Behn*, ed. Janet Todd (London: Macmillan Press, 1999).

Chibka, Robert, ' "Oh! Do Not Fear a Woman's Invention". Truth, falsehood, and fiction in Aphra Behn's *Oroonoko*', *Tulsa Studies in Literature and Language*, 30 (1988), pp. 510–37.

Ferguson, Margaret. 'Juggling the categories of race, class, and gender: Aphra Behn's *Oroonoko*', *Women's Studies*, 19 (1991), pp. 159–81; reprinted in *The New Casebooks. Aphra Behn*.

—, 'Feathers and flies: Aphra Behn and the seventeenth-century trade in exotica', in *Subject and Object in Renaissance Culture*, ed. by Margreta de Grazia, Maureen Quilligan and Peter Stallybrass (Cambridge: Cambridge University Press, 1996).

Ferguson, Moira, *Subject to Others: British Women Writers and Colonial Slavery, 1670–1834* (New York: Routledge, 1992).

Frohock, Richard, 'Violence and Awe: The Foundations of Government in Aphra Behn's New World Settings', *Eighteenth-Century Fiction*, 8 (1996), pp. 437–52.

Gallagher, Catherine, 'Oroonoko's Blackness', in *Aphra Behn*

Studies, ed. Janet Todd (Cambridge: Cambridge University Press, 1996).

Houston, Beverley, 'Usurpation and Dismemberment: Oedipal Tyranny in *Oroonoko*', *Literature and Psychology*, 32 (1986), pp. 30–36.

Hughes, Derek, 'Race, Gender, and Scholarly Practice: Aphra Behn's *Oroonoko*', *Essays in Criticism*, 52 (2002), pp. 1–22.

Lipking, Joanna, 'Confusing matters: searching the backgrounds of *Oroonoko*', in *Aphra Behn Studies*, ed. Todd.

Pacheco, Anita, 'Royalism and Honour in Aphra Behn's *Oroonoko*', *Studies in English Literature, 1500–1900* (1994), pp. 491–506.

Pearson, Jacqueline, 'Gender and narrative in the fiction of Aphra Behn', *Review of English Studies*, 42, nos. 165–6 (1991), pp. 40–56 and pp. 179–90; reprinted in *The New Casebooks. Aphra Behn*.

—, 'Slave princes and lady monsters: gender and ethnic difference in the work of Aphra Behn', *Aphra Behn Studies*.

Salzman, Paul, *English Prose Fiction 1558–1700* (Oxford: Clarendon Press, 1985).

Spencer, Jane, *Aphra Behn's Afterlife* (Oxford: Oxford University Press, 2000).

Starr, G. A., 'Aphra Behn and the Genealogy of the Man of Feeling', *Modern Philology* (May 1990), pp. 362–73.

Sussman, Charlotte, 'The Other Problem with Women: Reproduction and Slave Culture in Aphra Behn's *Oroonoko*', in *Rereading Aphra Behn: History, Theory, and Criticism*, ed. Heidi Hutner (Charlottesville: University Press of Virginia, 1993).

Todd, Janet, *The Critical Fortunes of Aphra Behn* (Columbia, SC: Camden House, 1998).

—, 'Spectacular deaths: history and story in Aphra Behn's *Love-Letters, Oroonoko* and *The Widow Ranter*', in *Gender, Art and Death* (Cambridge: Polity Press, 1993).

Zimbardo, Rose, 'Aphra Behn in Search of a Novel', *Studies in Eighteenth-Century Culture*, 19 (1989), pp. 277–87.

A Note on the Text

I have used as the basis for this edition the first printed version of *Oroonoko* published on its own in 1688, with the exception of the passage in the dedication to Lord Maitland beginning 'Where is it amongst all our nobility' and concluding with 'you convince the faithless and instruct the ignorant!'. This is a stop-press variant only existing in the Bodleian Library, Oxford, copy of *Oroonoko* as it was published in Aphra Behn's *Three Histories* (1688), a binding together of her first three published novels. For a more detailed description of the Bodleian text and the other early issues and editions of *Oroonoko*, see Mary Ann O'Donnell, *Aphra Behn: An Annotated Bibliography* (1986), pp. 140–48.

It was common seventeenth-century practice to vary type for effect and emphasis, with proper names and important passages in italics, and nouns and other parts of speech frequently capitalized. Spelling often differs from modern spelling and is inconsistent across a work, and punctuation occasionally obscures meaning for a modern reader. Since this is an edition for the general reader I have silently regularized spelling (for example, 'president' in the dedication has been amended to 'precedent'); I have also modernized punctuation where necessary, retaining commas before indirect speech for easier reading, and removing full stops after 'Mr' and 'St'. I have avoided capitalization and typographical extravagancies, although I have kept italics for direct speech. I have not, however, altered words in the original except where the sense demanded it; these occasions have either been marked with square brackets or recorded in the endnotes. Original quotations in the notes remain unchanged.

Oroonoko,
or
the Royal Slave

A True History

THE EPISTLE DEDICATORY

To the
Right Honourable
the
Lord Maitland.[1]

My Lord,

Since the world is grown so nice[2] and critical upon dedications, and will needs be judging the book by the wit of the patron, we ought, with a great deal of circumspection, to choose a person against whom there can be no exception; and whose wit and worth truly merits all that one is capable of saying upon that occasion.

The most part of dedications are charged with flattery; and if the world knows a man has some vices, they will not allow one to speak of his virtues. This, my Lord, is for want of thinking rightly; if men would consider with reason, they would have another sort of opinion and esteem of dedications, and would believe almost every great man has enough to make him worthy of all that can be said of him there. My Lord, a picture-drawer, when he intends to make a good picture, essays the face many ways and in many lights before he begins; that he may choose, from the several turns of it, which is most agreeable, and gives it the best grace; and if there be a scar, an ungrateful mole, or any little defect, they leave it out, and yet make the picture extremely like. But he who has the good fortune to draw a face that is exactly charming in all its parts and features, what colours or agreements[3] can be added to make it finer? All that he can give is but its due, and glories in a piece whose original alone gives it its perfection. An ill hand may diminish, but a good hand cannot augment its beauty. A poet is a painter in his way, he draws to the life, but in another kind; we draw the nobler part, the soul and mind; the pictures of the pen shall outlast those of the pencil, and even worlds themselves. It is a short

chronicle of those lives that possibly would be forgotten by
other historians, or lie neglected there, however deserving an
immortal fame; for men of eminent parts are as exemplary as
even monarchs themselves, and virtue is a noble lesson to be
learnt, and it is by comparison we can judge and choose. It is
by such illustrious precedents as your lordship the world can be
bettered and refined; when a great part of the lazy nobility shall,
with shame, behold the admirable accomplishments of a man
so great, and so young.

Your Lordship has read innumerable volumes of men and
books, not vainly for the gust[4] of novelty, but knowledge, excellent knowledge: like the industrious bee, from every flower you
return laden with the precious dew, which you are sure to turn
to the public good. You hoard no one perfection, but lay it all
out in the glorious service of your religion and country, to both
which you are a useful and necessary honour. They both want
such supporters, and it is only men of so elevated parts[5] and fine
knowledge, such noble principles of loyalty and religion this
nation sighs for. Where is it amongst all our nobility we shall
find so great a champion for the Catholic Church? With what
divine knowledge have you writ in defence of the faith! How
unanswerably have you cleared all these intricacies in religion,
which even the gownmen[6] have left dark and difficult! With
what unbeaten arguments you convince the faithless and
instruct the ignorant![7] Where shall we find a man so young, like
St Augustine,[8] in the midst of all his youth and gaiety, teaching
the world divine precepts, true notions of faith, and excellent
morality, and, at the same time, be also a perfect pattern of all
that accomplish a great man? You have, my Lord, all that refined
wit that charms and the affability that obliges; a generosity that
gives a lustre to your nobility, that hospitality and greatness of
mind that engages the world, and that admirable conduct that
so well instructs it. Our nation ought to regret and bemoan their
misfortunes for not being able to claim the honour of the birth
of a man who is so fit to serve his majesty and his kingdoms in
all great and public affairs. And to the glory of your nation be
it spoken, it produces more considerable men for all fine sense,

*wit, wisdom, breeding and generosity (for the generality of the
nobility) than all other nations can boast; and the fruitfulness
of your virtues sufficiently make amends for the barrenness
of your soil, which however cannot be incommode⁹ to your
Lordship, since your quality, and the veneration that the
commonality naturally pay their lords, creates a flowing plenty
there – that makes you happy. And to complete your happiness,
my Lord, heaven has blessed you with a lady to whom it has
given all the graces, beauties and virtues of her sex, all the youth,
sweetness of nature, of a most illustrious family;¹⁰ and who is a
most rare example to all wives of quality for her eminent piety,
easiness and condescension, and as absolutely merits respect
from all the world as she does that passion and resignation she
receives from your Lordship, and which is on her part with so
much tenderness returned. Methinks your tranquil lives are an
image of the new made and beautiful pair in paradise. And it is
the prayers and wishes of all who have the honour to know you
that it may eternally so continue, with additions of all the
blessings this world can give you.*

*My Lord, the obligations I have to some of the great men of
your nation, particularly to your Lordship, gives me an ambition
of making my acknowledgments by all the opportunities I can;
and such humble fruits as my industry produces I lay at your
Lordship's feet. This is a true story of a man gallant enough to
merit your protection; and, had he always been so fortunate, he
had not made so inglorious an end. The royal slave I had the
honour to know in my travels to the other world; and though I
had none above me in that country, yet I wanted power to
preserve this great man. If there be anything that seems romantic, I beseech your Lordship to consider, these countries do, in
all things, so far differ from ours that they produce inconceivable
wonders; at least they appear so to us because new and strange.
What I have mentioned I have taken care should be truth, let the
critical reader judge as he pleases. It will be no commendation to
the book to assure your Lordship I writ it in a few hours, though
it may serve to excuse some of its faults of connection; for I
never rested my pen a moment for thought. It is purely the merit*

of my slave that must render it worthy of the honour it begs,
and the author of that of subscribing herself,

My Lord,
your Lordship's most obliged and obedient servant,
A. Behn.

Oroonoko,
or
the Royal Slave

A True History

THE HISTORY
OF
THE ROYAL SLAVE

I do not pretend, in giving you the history of this royal slave, to entertain my reader with the adventures of a feigned hero whose life and fortunes fancy may manage at the poet's pleasure; nor in relating the truth, design to adorn it with any accidents but such as arrived in earnest to him. And it shall come simply into the world, recommended by its own proper merits and natural intrigues; there being enough of reality to support it and to render it diverting without the addition of invention.[1]

I was myself an eye-witness to a great part of what you will find here set down;[2] and what I could not be witness of I received from the mouth of the chief actor in this history, the hero himself, who gave us the whole transactions of his youth; and though I shall omit for brevity's sake a thousand little accidents of his life, which, however pleasant to us, where history was scarce and adventures very rare, yet might prove tedious and heavy to my reader in a world where he finds diversions for every minute, new and strange. But we who were perfectly charmed with the character of this great man, were curious to gather every circumstance of his life.

The scene of the last part of his adventures lies in a colony in America called Surinam[3] in the West Indies.

But before I give you the story of this gallant slave, it is fit I tell you the manner of bringing them to these new colonies; for those they make use of there are not natives of the place; for those we live with in perfect amity, without daring to command them, but on the contrary caress them with all the brotherly and friendly affection in the world; trading with them for their fish, venison, buffaloes, skins and little rarities, as marmosets, a

sort of monkey, as big as a rat or weasel, but of a marvellous
and delicate shape, and has face and hands like an human
creature; and *cousheries*,[4] a little beast in the form and fashion
of a lion, as big as a kitten, but so exactly made in all parts like
that noble beast, that it is it in miniature. Then for little para-
keets, great parrots, macaw, and a thousand other birds and
beasts of wonderful and surprising forms, shapes and colours.[5]
For skins of prodigious snakes, of which there are some three-
score yards in length, as is the skin of one that may be seen at
his Majesty's Antiquaries,[6] where are also some rare flies[7] of
amazing forms and colours, presented to them by myself, some
as big as my fist, some less, and all of various excellencies, such
as art cannot imitate. Then we trade for feathers, which they
order into all shapes, make themselves little short habits of
them, and glorious wreaths for their heads, necks, arms, and
legs, whose tinctures are inconceivable. I had a set of these
presented to me, and I gave them to the King's Theatre,[8] and it
was the dress of the *Indian Queen*,[9] infinitely admired by persons
of quality, and were inimitable. Besides these, a thousand little
knacks and rarities in nature, and some of art, as their baskets,
weapons, aprons, *etc.* We dealt with them with beads of all
colours, knives, axes, pins and needles, which they used only as
tools to drill holes with in their ears, noses and lips, where they
hang a great many little things, as long beads, bits of tin, brass
or silver beat thin, and any shining trinket. The beads they
weave into aprons about a quarter of an ell[10] long, and of the
same breadth, working them very prettily in flowers of several
colours of beads; which apron they wear just before them, as
Adam and Eve did the fig-leaves, the men wearing a long strip
of linen, which they deal with us for. They thread these beads
also on long cotton threads and make girdles to tie their aprons
to, which come twenty times or more about the waist, and then
cross like a shoulder-belt both ways, and round their necks,
arms and legs. This adornment, with their long black hair, and
the face painted in little specks or flowers here and there, makes
them a wonderful figure to behold. Some of the beauties which
indeed are finely shaped, as almost all are, and who have pretty
features, are very charming and novel, for they have all that is

called beauty, except the colour, which is a reddish yellow or after a new oiling, which they often use to themselves, they are of the colour of a new brick, but smooth, soft and sleek. They are extreme modest and bashful, very shy and nice of being touched. And though they are all thus naked, if one lives forever among them, there is not to be seen an indecent action or glance; and being continually used to see one another so unadorned,[11] so like our first parents before the Fall,[12] it seems as if they had no wishes, there being nothing to heighten curiosity, but all you can see, you see at once, and every moment see; and where there is no novelty, there can be no curiosity. Not but I have seen a handsome young Indian dying for love of a very beautiful young Indian maid; but all his courtship was to fold his arms, pursue her with his eyes, and sighs were all his language, while she, as if no such lover were present, or rather as if she desired none such, carefully guarded her eyes from beholding him and never approached him, but she looked down with all the blushing modesty I have seen in the most severe and cautious of our world. And these people represented to me an absolute idea of the first state of innocence, before man knew how to sin; and it is most evident and plain that simple Nature is the most harmless, inoffensive and virtuous mistress. It is she alone, if she were permitted, that better instructs the world than all the inventions of man; religion would here but destroy that tranquillity they possess by ignorance, and laws would but teach them to know offence, of which now they have no notion. They once made mourning and fasting for the death of the English governor who had given his hand to come on such a day to them, and neither came nor sent, believing, when once a man's word was past, nothing but death could or should prevent his keeping it. And when they saw he was not dead, they asked him, what name they had for a man who promised a thing he did not do? The governor told them, such a man was a liar, which was a word of infamy to a gentleman. Then one of them replied, *Governor, you are a liar, and guilty of that infamy*. They have a native justice, which knows no fraud;[13] and they understand no vice or cunning, but when they are taught by the white men. They have plurality of wives, which, when they grow old, they serve those that succeed them, who are young, but with a servitude easy and respected; and unless they take slaves in war, they have no other attendants.

Those on that continent where I was had no king, but the oldest war captain was obeyed with great resignation.

A war captain is a man who has led them on to battle with conduct[14] and success; of whom I shall have occasion to speak more hereafter, and of some other of their customs and manners, as they fall in my way.

With these people, as I said, we live in perfect tranquillity and good understanding,[15] as it behoves us to do, they knowing all the places where to seek the best food of the country and the means of getting it; and for very small and invaluable trifles, supply us with what it is impossible for us to get, for they do not only in the wood, and over the savannahs,[16] in hunting, supply the parts of hounds by swiftly scouring through those almost impassable places, and by the mere activity of their feet run down the nimblest deer and other eatable beasts, but in the water, one would think they were gods of the rivers, or fellow-citizens of the deep, so rare an art they have in swimming, diving and almost living in water, by which they command the less swift inhabitants of the floods. And then for shooting, what they cannot take or reach with their hands, they do with arrows, and have so admirable an aim that they will split almost an hair; and at any distance that an arrow can reach they will shoot down oranges and other fruit, and only touch the stalk with the darts' points that they may not hurt the fruit. So that they being, on all occasions very useful to us, we find it absolutely necessary to caress them as friends, and not to treat them as slaves; nor dare we do other, their numbers so far surpassing ours[17] in that continent.

Those then whom we make use of to work in our plantations of sugar are Negroes, black slaves altogether, which are transported thither in this manner.

Those who want slaves make a bargain with a master or a captain of a ship, and contract to pay him so much apiece, a matter of twenty pound a head for as many as he agrees for, and to pay for them when they shall be delivered on such a plantation. So that when there arrives a ship laden with slaves, they who have so contracted go aboard and receive their number by lot;[18] and perhaps in one lot that may be for ten, there may happen to be three or four men, the rest women and children; or be there more or less of either sex, you are obliged to be contented with your lot.

Coramantien,[19] a country of blacks so called, was one of those places in which they found the most advantageous trading for these slaves, and thither most of our great traders in that merchandise trafficked; for that nation is very warlike and brave, and having a continual campaign, being always in hostility with one neighbouring prince or other, they had the fortune to take a great many captives; for all they took in battle were sold as slaves, at least those common men who could not ransom themselves. Of these slaves so taken, the general only has all the profit; and of these generals, our captains and masters of ships buy all their freights.

The king of Coramantien was himself a man of an hundred and odd years old, and had no son, though he had many beautiful black wives; for most certainly there are beauties that can charm of that colour. In his younger years he had had many gallant men to his sons, thirteen of which died in battle, conquering when they fell; and he had only left him for his successor one grandchild,[20] son to one of these dead victors, who, as soon as he could bear a bow in his hand and a quiver at his back, was sent into the field to be trained up by one of the oldest generals to war; where, from his natural inclination to arms and the occasions given him with the good conduct of the old general, he became, at the age of seventeen, one of the most expert captains and bravest soldiers that ever saw the field of Mars;[21] so that he was adored as the wonder of all that world and the darling of the soldiers. Besides, he was adorned with a native beauty so transcending all those of his gloomy race that he struck an awe and reverence, even in those that knew not his quality; as he did in me, who beheld him with surprise and wonder when afterwards he arrived in our world.

He had scarce arrived at his seventeenth year, when, fighting by his side, the general was killed with an arrow in his eye,

which the Prince Oroonoko[22] (for so was this gallant Moor[23]
called) very narrowly avoided; nor had he, if the general, who
saw the arrow shot and perceiving it aimed at the prince, had
not bowed his head between, on purpose to receive it in his own
body, rather than it should touch that of the prince, and so
saved him.

It was then, afflicted as Oroonoko was, that he was pro-
claimed general in the old man's place; and then it was, at the
finishing of that war, which had continued for two years, that
the prince came to court, where he had hardly been a month
together, from the time of his fifth year to that of seventeen; and
it was amazing to imagine where it was he learned so much
humanity, or, to give his accomplishments a juster name, where
it was he got that real greatness of soul, those refined notions of
true honour, that absolute generosity, and that softness that was
capable of the highest passions of love and gallantry, whose
objects were almost continually fighting men, or those mangled
or dead, who heard no sounds but those of war and groans.
Some part of it we may attribute to the care of a Frenchman of
wit and learning, who finding it turn to very good account to be
a sort of royal tutor to this young black, and perceiving him
very ready, apt and quick of apprehension, took a great pleasure
to teach him morals, language and science, and was for it
extremely beloved and valued by him. Another reason was, he
loved, when he came from war, to see all the English gentlemen
that traded thither; and did not only learn their language, but
that of the Spaniards[24] also, with whom he traded afterwards
for slaves.

I have often seen and conversed with this great man, and been
a witness to many of his mighty actions; and do assure my
reader, the most illustrious courts could not have produced a
braver man, both for greatness of courage and mind, a judge-
ment more solid, a wit more quick and a conversation more
sweet and diverting. He knew almost as much as if he had read
much: he had heard of and admired the Romans; he had heard
of the late Civil Wars in England and the deplorable death
of our great monarch,[25] and would discourse of it with all the
sense and abhorrence of the injustice imaginable. He had an

extreme good and graceful mien and all the civility of a well-bred great man. He had nothing of barbarity in his nature, but in all points addressed himself as if his education had been in some European court.

This great and just character of Oroonoko gave me an extreme curiosity to see him, especially when I knew he spoke French and English, and that I could talk with him. But though I had heard so much of him, I was as greatly surprised when I saw him as if I had heard nothing of him, so beyond all report I found him. He came into the room, and addressed himself to me and some other women with the best grace in the world. He was pretty tall, but of a shape the most exact that can be fancied; the most famous statuary[26] could not form the figure of a man more admirably turned from head to foot. His face was not of that brown, rusty black which most of that nation are, but a perfect ebony or polished jet. His eyes were the most awful[27] that could be seen, and very piercing; the white of them being like snow, as were his teeth. His nose was rising and Roman instead of African and flat. His mouth, the finest shaped that could be seen, far from those great turned lips which are so natural to the rest of the Negroes. The whole proportion and air of his face was so noble and exactly formed that, bating[28] his colour, there could be nothing in nature more beautiful, agreeable and handsome.[29] There was no one grace wanting that bears the standard of true beauty. His hair came down to his shoulders by the aids of art, which was, by pulling it out with a quill and keeping it combed, of which he took particular care. Nor did the perfections of his mind come short of those of his person; for his discourse was admirable upon almost any subject, and whoever had heard him speak would have been convinced of their errors that all fine wit is confined to the white men, especially to those of Christendom; and would have confessed that Oroonoko was as capable even of reigning well, and of governing as wisely, had as great a soul, as politic[30] maxims, and was as sensible of power as any prince civilized in the most refined schools of humanity and learning, or the most illustrious courts.

This prince, such as I have described him, whose soul and

body were so admirably adorned, was (while yet he was in the court of his grandfather) as I said, as capable of love as it was possible for a brave and gallant man to be; and in saying that, I have named the highest degree of love; for sure, great souls are most capable of that passion.

I have already said the old general was killed by the shot of an arrow, by the side of this prince, in battle, and that Oroonoko was made general. This old dead hero had one only daughter left of his race; a beauty that, to describe her truly, one need say only, she was female to the noble male, the beautiful black Venus to our young Mars,[31] as charming in her person as he, and of delicate virtues. I have seen an hundred white men sighing after her and making a thousand vows at her feet, all vain and unsuccessful; and she was, indeed, too great for any but a prince of her own nation to adore.

Oroonoko coming from the wars (which were now ended), after he had made his court to his grandfather, he thought in honour he ought to make a visit to Imoinda, the daughter of his foster-father, the dead general; and to make some excuses to her, because his preservation was the occasion of her father's death; and to present her with those slaves that had been taken in this last battle, as the trophies of her father's victories. When he came, attended by all the young soldiers of any merit, he was infinitely surprised at the beauty of this fair Queen of Night, whose face and person was so exceeding all he had ever beheld; that lovely modesty with which she received him, that softness in her look and sighs upon the melancholy occasion of this honour that was done by so great a man as Oroonoko, and a prince of whom she had heard such admirable things; the awfulness[32] wherewith she received him, and the sweetness of her words and behaviour while he stayed, gained a perfect conquest over his fierce heart, and made him feel the victor could be subdued. So that having made his first compliments and presented her a hundred and fifty slaves in fetters, he told her with his eyes, that he was not insensible of her charms; while Imoinda, who wished for nothing more than so glorious a conquest, was pleased to believe she understood that silent language of new-born love; and from that moment put on all her additions to beauty.

The prince returned to court with quite another humour than before; and though he did not speak much of the fair Imoinda, he had the pleasure to hear all his followers speak of nothing but the charms of that maid; insomuch that, even in the presence of the old king, they were extolling her, and heightening, if possible, the beauties they had found in her; so that nothing else was talked of, no other sound was heard in every corner where there were whisperers, but *Imoinda! Imoinda!*

It will be imagined Oroonoko stayed not long before he made his second visit; nor, considering his quality, not much longer before he told her, he adored her. I have often heard him say that he admired[33] by what strange inspiration he came to talk things so soft, and so passionate, who never knew love, nor was used to the conversation[34] of women; but (to use his own words) he said, most happily, some new and till then unknown power instructed his heart and tongue in the language of love, and at the same time, in favour of him, inspired Imoinda with a sense of his passion. She was touched with what he said, and returned it all in such answers as went to his very heart, with a pleasure unknown before. Nor did he use those obligations ill that love had done him, but turned all his happy moments to the best advantage; and as he knew no vice, his flame aimed at nothing but honour, if such a distinction may be made in love; and especially in that country, where men take to themselves as many as they can maintain and where the only crime and sin with woman is to turn her off, to abandon her to want, shame and misery. Such ill morals are only practised in Christian countries, where they prefer the bare name of religion; and without virtue or morality think that is sufficient. But Oroonoko was none of those professors; but as he had right notions of honour, so he made her such propositions as were not only and barely such; but, contrary to the custom of his country, he made her vows she should be the only woman he would possess while he lived; that no age or wrinkles should incline him to change, for her soul would be always fine and always young; and he should have an eternal idea in his mind of the charms she now bore, and should look into his heart for that idea when he could find it no longer in her face.

After a thousand assurances of his lasting flame and her eternal empire over him, she condescended to receive him for her husband; or rather, received him as the greatest honour the gods[35] could do her.

There is a certain ceremony in these cases to be observed, which I forgot to ask how it was performed; but it was concluded on both sides that, in obedience to him, the grandfather was to be first made acquainted with the design; for they pay a most absolute resignation to the monarch, especially when he is a parent also.

On the other side, the old king, who had many wives and many concubines, wanted not court flatterers to insinuate in his heart a thousand tender thoughts for this young beauty, and who represented her to his fancy as the most charming he had ever possessed in all the long race of his numerous years. At this character, his old heart, like an extinguished brand, most apt to take fire, felt new sparks of love and began to kindle; and now grown to his second childhood, longed with impatience to behold this gay thing, with whom, alas, he could but innocently play. But how he should be confirmed she was this wonder, before he used his power to call her to court (where maidens never came, unless for the king's private use) he was next to consider; and while he was so doing, he had intelligence brought him that Imoinda was most certainly mistress to the Prince Oroonoko. This gave him some chagrin; however, it gave him also an opportunity, one day, when the prince was a-hunting, to wait on a man of quality as his slave and attendant, who should go and make a present to Imoinda as from the prince; he should then, unknown, see this fair maid and have an opportunity to hear what message she would return the prince for his present; and from thence gather the state of her heart and degree of her inclination. This was put in execution, and the old monarch saw, and burnt;[36] he found her all he had heard, and would not delay his happiness, but found he should have some obstacle to overcome her heart; for she expressed her sense of the present the prince had sent her in terms so sweet, so soft and pretty, with an air of love and joy that could not be dissembled, insomuch that it was past doubt whether she loved Oroonoko entirely. This gave the old king some affliction, but he salved it with this, that the obedience the people pay their king was not at all inferior to what they paid their gods, and what love would not oblige Imoinda to do, duty would compel her to.

He was therefore no sooner got to his apartment, but he sent the royal veil to Imoinda, that is, the ceremony of invitation he sends the lady he has a mind to honour with his bed; a veil, with which she is covered and secured for the king's use; and it is death to disobey, besides, held a most impious disobedience.

It is not to be imagined the surprise and grief that seized this lovely maid at this news and sight. However, as delays in these cases are dangerous and pleading worse than treason, trembling and almost fainting she was obliged to suffer herself to be covered and led away.

They brought her thus to court; and the king, who had caused a very rich bath to be prepared, was led into it, where he sat under a canopy in state, to receive this longed for virgin; whom he having commanded should be brought to him, they (after disrobing her) led her to the bath, and making fast the doors, left her to descend. The king, without more courtship, bade her throw off her mantle and come to his arms. But Imoinda, all in tears, threw herself on the marble on the brink of the bath and besought him to hear her. She told him, as she was a maid, how proud of the divine glory she should have been of having it in her power to oblige her king; but as by the laws he could not, and from his royal goodness would not take from any man his wedded wife, so she believed she should be the occasion of making him commit a great sin if she did not reveal her state and condition, and tell him she was another's and could not be so happy to be his.

The king, enraged at this delay, hastily demanded the name of the bold man that had married a woman of her degree without his consent. Imoinda, seeing his eyes fierce and his hands tremble, whether with age or anger I know not, but she fancied the last, almost repented she had said so much, for now she feared the storm would fall on the prince; she therefore said a thousand things to appease the raging of his flame, and to prepare him to hear who it was with calmness; but before she spoke, he imagined who she meant, but would not seem to do so, but commanded her to lay aside her mantle and suffer herself to receive his caresses, or, by his gods, he swore, that happy man whom she was going to name should die, though it were even Oroonoko himself. *Therefore*, said he, *deny this marriage and swear thyself a maid. That*, replied Imoinda, *by all our powers I do, for I am not yet known to my husband. It is enough*, said the king, *it is enough both to satisfy my conscience and my heart.* And rising from his seat, he went and led her into the bath, it being in vain for her to resist.

In this time the prince, who was returned from hunting, went to visit his Imoinda, but found her gone; and not only so, but heard she had received the royal veil. This raised him to a storm, and in his madness they had much ado to save him from laying violent hands on himself. Force first prevailed, and then reason. They urged all to him that might oppose his rage; but nothing weighed so greatly with him as the king's old age, incapable of injuring him[37] with Imoinda. He would give way to that hope, because it pleased him most and flattered best his heart. Yet this served not altogether to make him cease his different passions, which sometimes raged within him, and sometimes softened into showers. It was not enough to appease him, to tell him his grandfather was old and could not that way injure him, while he retained that awful duty which the young men are used there to pay to their grave relations. He could not be convinced he had no cause to sigh and mourn for the loss of a mistress he could not with all his strength and courage retrieve. And he would often cry, *O, my friends! were she in walled cities, or confined from me in fortifications of the greatest strength; did enchantments or monsters detain her from me, I would venture through any hazard to free her. But here, in the arms of a feeble old man, my youth, my violent love, my trade in arms, and all my vast desire of glory avail me nothing. Imoinda is as irrecoverably lost to me as if she were snatched by the cold arms of death. Oh! she is never to be retrieved. If I would wait tedious*

years, till fate should bow the old king to his grave, even that
would not leave me Imoinda free; but still that custom that
makes it so vile a crime for a son to marry his father's wives or
mistresses would hinder my happiness; unless I would either
ignobly set an ill precedent to my successors, or abandon my
country and fly with her to some unknown world who never
heard our story.

But it was objected[38] to him, that his case was not the same;
for Imoinda being his lawful wife by solemn contract, it was he
was the injured man, and might, if he so pleased, take Imoinda
back, the breach of the law being on his grandfather's side; and
that if he could circumvent him and redeem her from the *otan*,[39]
which is the palace of the king's women, a sort of seraglio, it
was both just and lawful for him so to do.

This reasoning had some force upon him, and he should
have been entirely comforted, but for the thought that she was
possessed by his grandfather. However, he loved so well that he
was resolved to believe what most favoured his hope, and to
endeavour to learn from Imoinda's own mouth, what only she
could satisfy him in: whether she was robbed of that blessing
which was only due to his faith and love. But as it was very hard
to get a sight of the women, for no men ever entered into the
otan, but when the king went to entertain himself with some
one of his wives or mistresses, and it was death at any other
time for any other to go in, so he knew not how to contrive to
get a sight of her.

While Oroonoko felt all the agonies of love and suffered
under a torment the most painful in the world, the old king was
not exempted from his share of affliction. He was troubled for
having been forced by an irresistible passion to rob his son[40] of
a treasure he knew could not but be extremely dear to him, since
she was the most beautiful that ever had been seen, and had
besides all the sweetness and innocence of youth and modesty,
with a charm of wit surpassing all. He found that however she
was forced to expose her lovely person to his withered arms,
she could only sigh and weep there and think of Oroonoko; and
oftentimes could not forbear speaking of him, though her life
were, by custom, forfeited by owning her passion. But she spoke

not of a lover only, but of a prince dear to him to whom she spoke; and of the praises of a man, who, till now, filled the old man's soul with joy at every recital of his bravery, or even his name. And it was this dotage on our young hero that gave Imoinda a thousand privileges to speak of him without offending; and this condescension in the old king that made her take the satisfaction of speaking of him so very often.

Besides, he many times enquired how the prince bore himself; and those of whom he asked, being entirely slaves to the merits and virtues of the prince, still answered what they thought conduced best to his service; which was, to make the old king fancy that the prince had no more interest in Imoinda and had resigned her willingly to the pleasure of the king; that he diverted himself with his mathematicians, his fortifications, his officers and his hunting.

This pleased the old lover, who failed not to report these things again to Imoinda, that she might, by the example of her young lover, withdraw her heart and rest better contented in his arms. But however she was forced to receive this unwelcome news, in all appearance, with unconcern and content, her heart was bursting within and she was only happy when she could get alone, to vent her griefs and moans with sighs and tears.

What reports of the prince's conduct were made to the king, he thought good to justify as far as possibly he could by his actions; and when he appeared in the presence of the king, he showed a face not at all betraying his heart, so that in a little time the old man, being entirely convinced that he was no longer a lover of Imoinda, he carried him with him in his train to the *otan*, often to banquet with his mistress. But as soon as he entered, one day, into the apartment of Imoinda with the king, at the first glance from her eyes, notwithstanding all his determined resolution, he was ready to sink in the place where he stood; and had certainly done so, but for the support of Aboan, a young man who was next to him; which, with his change of countenance, had betrayed him, had the king chanced to look that way. And I have observed, it is a very great error in those who laugh when one says, *a Negro can change colour*; for I have seen them as frequently blush and look pale, and that as visibly as ever I saw in the most beautiful white. And it is certain that both these changes were evident, this day, in both these lovers. And Imoinda, who saw with some joy the change in the prince's face, and found it in her own, strove to divert the king from beholding either by a forced caress, with which she met him, which was a new wound in the heart of the poor dying prince. But as soon as the king was busied in looking on some fine thing of Imoinda's making, she had time to tell the prince with her angry but love-darting eyes that she resented his coldness and bemoaned her own miserable captivity. Nor were his eyes silent, but answered hers again, as much as eyes could do, instructed by the most tender and most passionate heart that ever loved. And they spoke so well and so effectually, as Imoinda no longer doubted but she was the only delight and the darling of that soul she found pleading in them its right of love, which none was more willing to resign than she. And it was this powerful language alone that in an instant conveyed all the thoughts of their souls to each other, that they both found there wanted but opportunity to make them both entirely happy. But when he saw another door opened by Onahal, a former old wife of the king's, who now had charge of Imoinda, and saw the prospect of a bed of state made ready with sweets and flowers for the dalliance of the king, who immediately led the trembling victim from his sight into that prepared repose, what rage, what wild frenzies seized his heart! Which forcing to keep within bounds and to suffer without noise, it became the more insupportable and rent his soul with ten thousand pains. He was forced to retire to vent his groans, where he fell down on a carpet and lay struggling a long time, and only breathing now and then, *O Imoinda!* When Onahal had finished her necessary affair within, shutting the door, she came forth to wait till the king called; and hearing someone sighing in the other room, she passed on and found the prince in that deplorable condition which she thought needed her aid. She gave him cordials, but all in vain; till finding the nature of his disease, by his sighs and naming Imoinda, she told him, he had not so much cause as he imagined to afflict himself, for if he knew the king so well as she did, he would not lose a moment in jealousy, and that she was confident that Imoinda bore, at this moment, part in his affliction. Aboan was of the same opinion, and both together persuaded him to reassume his courage; and all sitting down on the carpet, the prince said so many obliging things to Onahal that he half persuaded her to be of his party. And she promised him she would thus far comply with his just desires, that she would let Imoinda know how faithful he was, what he suffered and what he said.

This discourse lasted till the king called, which gave Oroonoko a certain satisfaction; and with the hope Onahal had made him conceive, he assumed a look as gay as it was possible a man in his circumstances could do; and presently after, he was called in with the rest who waited without. The king commanded music to be brought, and several of his young wives and mistresses came all together by his command, to dance before him; where Imoinda performed her part with an air and grace so passing all the rest as her beauty was above them, and received the present, ordained as a prize. The prince was every moment more charmed with the new beauties and graces he beheld in this fair one; and while he gazed and she danced, Onahal was retired to a window with Aboan.

This Onahal, as I said, was one of the cast mistresses[41] of the old king; and it was these (now past their beauty) that were made guardians or governants[42] to the new and the young ones; and whose business it was to teach them all those wanton arts of love with which they prevailed and charmed heretofore in their turn; and who now treated the triumphing happy ones with all the severity, as to liberty and freedom, that was possible, in revenge of those honours they rob them of, envying them those satisfactions, those gallantries and presents, that were once made to themselves while youth and beauty lasted, and which they now saw pass regardless by, and paid only to the bloomings. And certainly, nothing is more afflicting to a decayed beauty than to behold in itself declining charms that were once adored, and to find those caresses paid to new beauties to which once she laid a claim; to hear them whisper as she passes by, *that once was a delicate woman*. These abandoned ladies therefore endeavour to revenge all the despites[43] and decays of time on these flourishing happy ones. And it was this severity that gave Oroonoko a thousand fears he should never prevail with Onahal to see Imoinda. But, as I said, she was now retired to a window with Aboan.

This young man was not only one of the best quality, but a man extremely well made and beautiful; and coming often to attend the king to the *otan*, he had subdued the heart of the antiquated Onahal, which had not forgot how pleasant it was to be in love. And though she had some decays in her face, she had none in her sense and wit; she was there agreeable still, even to Aboan's youth, so that he took pleasure in entertaining her with discourses of love. He knew also, that to make his court to these she-favourites was the way to be great, these being the persons that do all affairs and business at court. He had also observed that she had given him glances more tender and inviting than she had done to others of his quality. And now, when he saw that her favour could so absolutely oblige the prince, he failed not to sigh in her ear, and to look with eyes all soft upon her, and give her hope that she had made some impressions on his heart. He found her pleased at this, and making a thousand advances to him; but the ceremony ending and the king departing broke up the company for that day, and his conversation.

Aboan failed not that night to tell the prince of his success, and how advantageous the service of Onahal might be to his amour with Imoinda. The prince was overjoyed with this good news and besought him, if it were possible, to caress her, so as to engage her entirely, which he could not fail to do if he complied with her desires. *For then*, said the prince, *her life lying at your mercy, she must grant you the request you make in my behalf*. Aboan understood him and assured him, he would make love so effectually that he would defy the most expert mistress of the art to find out whether he dissembled it or had it really. And it was with impatience they waited the next opportunity of going to the *otan*.

The wars came on, the time of taking the field approached, and it was impossible for the prince to delay his going at the head of his army to encounter the enemy; so that every day seemed a tedious year till he saw his Imoinda, for he believed he could not live if he were forced away without being so happy. It was with impatience therefore, that he expected the next visit the king would make and, according to his wish, it was not long.

The parley of the eyes of these two lovers had not passed so secretly, but an old jealous lover could spy it; or rather, he wanted not flatterers who told him they observed it. So that the prince was hastened to the camp, and this was the last visit he found he should make to the *otan*; he therefore urged Aboan to make the best of this last effort, and to explain himself so to Onahal, that she, deferring her enjoyment of her young lover no longer, might make way for the prince to speak to Imoinda.

The whole affair being agreed on between the prince and Aboan, they attended the king, as the custom was, to the *otan*; where, while the whole company was taken up in beholding the dancing and antic[44] postures the women royal made to divert the king, Onahal singled out Aboan, whom she found most pliable to her wish. When she had him where she believed she could not be heard, she sighed to him and softly cried, *Ah, Aboan! When will you be sensible of my passion? I confess it with my mouth, because I would not give my eyes the lie, and you have but too much already perceived they have confessed my flame. Nor would I have you believe that, because I am the abandoned mistress of a king, I esteem myself altogether divested of charms. No, Aboan, I have still a rest*[45] *of beauty enough engaging, and have learned to please too well, not to be desirable. I can have lovers still, but will have none but Aboan. Madam*, replied the half-feigning youth, *you have already by my eyes found you can still conquer; and I believe it is in pity of me you condescend to this kind confession. But, Madam, words are used to be so small a part of our country courtship that it is rare one can get so happy an opportunity as to tell one's heart; and those few minutes we have are forced to be snatched for more certain proofs of love than speaking and sighing, and such I languish for.*

He spoke this with such a tone that she hoped it true and could not forbear believing it; and being wholly transported with joy, for having subdued the finest of all the king's subjects to her desires, she took from her ears two large pearls and commanded him to wear them in his. He would have refused them, crying, *Madam, these are not the proofs of your love that I expect; it is opportunity, it is a lone hour only, that can make me happy*. But forcing the pearls into his hand, she whispered softly to him, *Oh! Do not fear a woman's invention, when love sets her a-thinking*. And pressing his hand, she cried, *This night you shall be happy. Come to the gate of the orange groves behind the otan, and I will be ready about midnight to receive you*. It was thus agreed, and she left him, that no notice might be taken of their speaking together.

The ladies were still dancing, and the king, laid on a carpet, with a great deal of pleasure was beholding them, especially Imoinda, who that day appeared more lovely than ever, being enlivened with the good tidings Onahal had brought her of the constant passion the prince had for her. The prince was laid on another carpet, at the other end of the room, with his eyes fixed on the object of his soul; and as she turned or moved, so did they, and she alone gave his eyes and soul their motions. Nor did Imoinda employ her eyes to any other use than in beholding with infinite pleasure the joy she produced in those of the prince. But while she was more regarding him than the steps she took, she chanced to fall, and so near him as that leaping with extreme force from the carpet, he caught her in his arms as she fell; and it was visible to the whole presence, the joy wherewith he received her. He clasped her close to his bosom and quite forgot that reverence that was due to the mistress of a king, and that punishment that is the reward of a boldness of this nature; and had not the presence of mind of Imoinda (fonder of his safety than her own) befriended him in making her spring from his arms and fall into her dance again, he had, at that instant, met his death; for the old king, jealous to the last degree, rose up in rage, broke all the diversion and led Imoinda to her apartment, and sent out word to the prince to go immediately to the camp, and that if he were found another night in court, he should suffer the death ordained for disobedient offenders.

You may imagine how welcome this news was to Oroonoko, whose unseasonable transport and caress of Imoinda was blamed by all men that loved him; and now he perceived his fault, yet cried, that for such another moment he would be content to die.

All the *otan* was in disorder about this accident; and Onahal was particularly concerned, because on the prince's stay depended her happiness, for she could no longer expect that of Aboan. So that, ere they departed, they contrived it so that the prince and he should both come that night to the grove of the *otan*, which was all of oranges and citrons, and that there they would wait her orders.

They parted thus, with grief enough, till night; leaving the king in possession of the lovely maid. But nothing could appease the jealousy of the old lover; he would not be imposed on, but would have it that Imoinda made a false step on purpose to fall into Oroonoko's bosom, and that all things looked like a design on both sides, and it was in vain she protested her innocence. He was old and obstinate, and left her more than half assured that his fear was true.

The king going to his apartment, sent to know where the prince was, and if he intended to obey his command. The messenger returned and told him, he found the prince pensive and altogether unpreparing for the campaign; that he lay negligently on the ground and answered very little. This confirmed the jealousy of the king, and he commanded that they should very narrowly and privately watch his motions, and that he should not stir from his apartment, but one spy or other should be employed to watch him. So that the hour approaching wherein he was to go to the citron grove, and taking only Aboan along with him, he leaves his apartment, and was watched to the very gate of the *otan*, where he was seen to enter, and where they left him to carry back the tidings to the king.

Oroonoko and Aboan were no sooner entered but Onahal led the prince to the apartment of Imoinda, who, not knowing anything of her happiness, was laid in bed. But Onahal only left him in her chamber to make the best of his opportunity, and took her dear Aboan to her own, where he showed the height of complaisance for his prince, when, to give him an opportunity, he suffered himself to be caressed in bed by Onahal.

The prince softly wakened Imoinda, who was not a little surprised with joy to find him there, and yet she trembled with a thousand fears. I believe he omitted saying nothing to this young maid that might persuade her to suffer him to seize his own, and take the rights of love; and I believe she was not long resisting those arms where she so longed to be; and having opportunity, night and silence, youth, love and desire, he soon prevailed, and ravished in a moment what his old grandfather had been endeavouring for so many months.[46]

It is not to be imagined the satisfaction of these two young lovers; nor the vows she made him that she remained a spotless maid till that night; and that what she did with his grandfather had robbed him of no part of her virgin honour, the gods in mercy and justice having reserved that for her plighted lord, to whom of right it belonged. And it is impossible to express the transports he suffered, while he listened to a discourse so charming from her loved lips, and clasped that body in his arms for whom he had so long languished; and nothing now afflicted him but his sudden departure from her; for he told her the necessity and his commands, but should depart satisfied in this, that since the old king had hitherto not been able to deprive him of those enjoyments which only belonged to him, he believed for the future he would be less able to injure him. So that, abating the scandal of the veil, which was no otherwise so than that she was wife to another, he believed her safe, even in the arms of the king, and innocent; yet would he have ventured at the conquest of the world, and have given it all, to have had her avoided that honour of receiving the royal veil. It was thus, between a thousand caresses, that both bemoaned the hard fate of youth and beauty, so liable to that cruel promotion; it was a glory that could well have been spared here, though desired and aimed at by all the young females of that kingdom.

But while they were thus fondly employed, forgetting how time ran on, and that the dawn must conduct him far away from his only happiness, they heard a great noise in the *otan*, and unusual voices of men; at which the prince, starting from the arms of the frighted Imoinda, ran to a little battle-axe he used to wear by his side, and having not so much leisure as to put on his habit, he opposed himself against some who were already opening the door; which they did with so much violence, that Oroonoko was not able to defend it, but was forced to cry out with a commanding voice, *Whoever ye are that have the boldness to attempt to approach this apartment thus rudely, know that I, the Prince Oroonoko, will revenge it with the certain death of him that first enters. Therefore stand back, and know this place is sacred to love and me this night; tomorrow it is the king's.*

This he spoke with a voice so resolved and assured that they soon retired from the door, but cried, *It is by the king's command we are come; and being satisfied by thy voice, O Prince, as much as if we had entered, we can report to the king the truth of all his fears, and leave thee to provide for thy own safety, as thou art advised by thy friends.*

At these words they departed and left the prince to take a short and sad leave of his Imoinda; who trusting in the strength of her charms, believed she should appease the fury of a jealous king by saying she was surprised, and that it was by force of arms he got into her apartment. All her concern now was for his life, and therefore she hastened him to the camp, and with much ado prevailed on him to go. Nor was it she alone that prevailed; Aboan and Onahal both pleaded, and both assured him of a lie that should be well enough contrived to secure Imoinda. So that, at last, with a heart sad as death, dying eyes and sighing soul, Oroonoko departed and took his way to the camp.

It was not long after the king in person came to the *otan*, where beholding Imoinda with rage in his eyes, he upbraided her wickedness and perfidy, and threatening her royal lover; she fell on her face at his feet, bedewing the floor with her tears and imploring his pardon for a fault which she had not with her will committed, as Onahal, who was also prostrate with her, could testify, that, unknown to her, he had broke into her apartment and ravished her. She spoke this much against her conscience; but to save her own life, it was absolutely necessary she should feign this falsity. She knew it could not injure the prince, he being fled to an army that would stand by him against any injuries that should assault him. However, this last thought of Imoinda's being ravished changed the measures of his revenge, and whereas before he designed to be himself her executioner, he now resolved she should not die. But as it is the greatest crime in nature amongst them to touch a woman after having been possessed by a son, a father or a brother, so now he looked on Imoinda as a polluted thing, wholly unfit for his embrace; nor would he resign her to his grandson, because she had received the royal veil. He therefore removes her from the *otan*, with Onahal, whom he put into safe hands, with order they should be both sold off as slaves to another country, either Christian, or heathen, it was no matter where.

This cruel sentence, worse than death, they implored might be reversed; but their prayers were vain, and it was put in execution accordingly, and that with so much secrecy that none, either without or within the *otan*, knew anything of their absence or their destiny.

The old king, nevertheless, executed this with a great deal of reluctance; but he believed he had made a very great conquest over himself when he had once resolved, and had performed what he resolved. He believed now that his love had been unjust, and that he could not expect the gods, or Captain of the Clouds (as they call the unknown power) should suffer a better consequence from so ill a cause. He now begins to hold Oroonoko excused, and to say, he had reason for what he did; and now everybody could assure the king how passionately Imoinda was beloved by the prince, even those confessed it now who said the contrary before his flame was abated. So that the king being old and not able to defend himself in war, and having no sons of all his race remaining alive but only this to maintain him on his throne; and looking on this as a man disobliged,[47] first by the rape of his mistress, or rather wife, and now by depriving him wholly of her, he feared might make him desperate, and do some cruel thing, either to himself, or his old grandfather, the offender, he began to repent him[48] extremely of the contempt he had, in his rage, put on Imoinda. Besides, he considered he ought in honour to have killed her for this offence, if it had been one. He ought to have had so much value and consideration for a maid of her quality as to have nobly put her to death, and not to have sold her like a common slave, the greatest revenge, and the most disgraceful of any, and to which they a thousand times prefer death, and implore it as Imoinda did, but could not obtain that honour. Seeing therefore it was certain that Oroonoko would highly resent this affront, he thought good to make some excuse for his rashness to him, and to that end he sent a messenger to the camp with orders to treat with him about the matter, to gain his pardon, and to endeavour to mitigate his grief; but that by no means he should tell him she was sold, but secretly put to death, for he knew he should never obtain his pardon for the other.

When the messenger came, he found the prince upon the point of engaging with the enemy, but as soon as he heard of the arrival of the messenger he commanded him to his tent, where he embraced him and received him with joy; which was soon abated by the downcast looks of the messenger, who was instantly demanded the cause by Oroonoko, who, impatient of delay, asked a thousand questions in a breath, and all concerning Imoinda. But there needed little return, for he could almost answer himself of all he demanded from his sighs and eyes. At last, the messenger casting himself at the prince's feet and kissing them with all the submission of a man that had something to implore which he dreaded to utter, he besought him to hear with calmness what he had to deliver to him, and to call up all his noble and heroic courage to encounter with his words, and defend himself against the ungrateful things he must relate. Oroonoko replied, with a deep sigh and a languishing voice, *I am armed against their worst efforts – for I know they will tell me, Imoinda is no more – and after that, you may spare the rest.* Then, commanding him to rise, he laid himself on a carpet under a rich pavilion and remained a good while silent, and was hardly heard to sigh. When he was come a little to himself, the messenger asked him leave to deliver that part of his embassy which the prince had not yet divined, and the prince cried, *I permit thee.* Then he told him the affliction the old king was in for the rashness he had committed in his cruelty to Imoinda; and how he deigned to ask pardon for his offence, and to implore the prince would not suffer that loss to touch his heart too sensibly which now all the gods could not restore him, but might recompense him in glory, which he begged he would pursue; and that death, that common revenger of all injuries, would soon even the account between him and a feeble old man.

Oroonoko bade him return his duty to his lord and master, and to assure him there was no account of revenge to be adjusted between them; if there were, it was he was the aggressor, and that death would be just, and, maugre[49] his age, would see him righted; and he was contented to leave his share of glory to youths more fortunate and worthy of that favour from the gods. That henceforth he would never lift a weapon, or draw a bow, but abandon the small remains of his life to sighs and tears, and the continual thoughts of what his lord and grandfather had thought good to send out of the world with all that youth, that innocence and beauty.

After having spoken this, whatever his greatest officers and men of the best rank could do, they could not raise him from the carpet, or persuade him to action and resolutions of life; but commanding all to retire, he shut himself into his pavilion all that day, while the enemy was ready to engage; and wondering at the delay, the whole body of the chief of the army then addressed themselves to him, and to whom they had much ado to get admittance. They fell on their faces at the foot of his carpet, where they lay and besought him with earnest prayers and tears to lead them forth to battle, and not let the enemy take advantages of them, and implored him to have regard to his glory, and to the world that depended on his courage and conduct. But he made no other reply to all their supplications but this, that he had now no more business for glory, and, for the world, it was a trifle not worth his care. *Go*, continued he, sighing, *and divide it amongst you; and reap with joy what you so vainly prize, and leave me to my more welcome destiny.*

They then demanded, what they should do, and whom he would constitute[50] in his room, that the confusion of ambitious youth and power might not ruin their order, and make them a prey to the enemy. He replied, he would not give himself the trouble, but wished them to choose the bravest man amongst them, let his quality or birth be what it would; *For, O my friends!* said he, *it is not titles make men brave or good; or birth that bestows courage and generosity, or makes the owner happy. Believe this, when you behold Oroonoko, the most wretched and abandoned by fortune of all the creation of the gods.* So turning himself about, he would make no more reply to all they could urge or implore.

The army beholding their officers return unsuccessful, with sad faces and ominous looks that presaged no good luck, suffered a thousand fears to take possession of their hearts, and the enemy to come even upon them, before they would provide for their safety by any defence; and though they were assured by some who had a mind to animate them, that they should be immediately headed by the prince, and that in the meantime Aboan had orders to command as general, yet they were so dismayed for want of that great example of bravery that they could make but a very feeble resistance; and at last, downright fled before the enemy, who pursued them to the very tents, killing them. Nor could all Aboan's courage, which that day gained him immortal glory, shame them into a manly defence of themselves. The guards that were left behind about the prince's tent, seeing the soldiers flee before the enemy and scatter themselves all over the plain in great disorder, made such outcries as roused the prince from his amorous slumber, in which he had remained buried for two days without permitting any sustenance to approach him. But, in spite of all his resolutions, he had not the constancy of grief to that degree as to make him insensible of the danger of his army, and in that instant he leapt from his couch[51] and cried, *Come, if we must die, let us meet death the noblest way; and it will be more like Oroonoko to encounter him at an army's head, opposing the torrent of a conquering foe, than lazily on a couch to wait his lingering pleasure, and die every moment by a thousand wrecking[52] thought[s]; or be tamely taken by an enemy, and led a whining love-sick slave to adorn the triumphs of Jamoan, that young victor, who already is entered beyond the limits I had prescribed him.*

While he was speaking, he suffered his people to dress him

for the field; and sallying out of his pavilion, with more life and vigour in his countenance than ever he showed, he appeared like some divine power descended to save his country from destruction; and his people had purposely put on him[53] all things that might make him shine with most splendour, to strike a reverend awe into the beholders. He flew into the thickest of those that were pursuing his men, and being animated with despair, he fought as if he came on purpose to die, and did such things as will not be believed that human strength could perform, and such as soon inspired all the rest with new courage and new order. And now it was that they began to fight indeed, and so, as if they would not be outdone even by their adored hero, who turning the tide of the victory, changing absolutely the fate of the day, gained an entire conquest; and Oroonoko having the good fortune to single out Jamoan, he took him prisoner with his own hand, having wounded him almost to death.

This Jamoan afterwards became very dear to him, being a man very gallant and of excellent graces and fine parts; so that he never put him amongst the rank of captives, as they used to do, without distinction, for the common sale or market, but kept him in his own court, where he retained nothing of the prisoner but the name, and returned no more into his own country, so great an affection he took for Oroonoko; and by a thousand tales and adventures of love and gallantry, flattered his disease of melancholy and languishment, which I have often heard him say had certainly killed him, but for the conversation of this prince and Aboan, [and] the French governor he had from his childhood, of whom I have spoken before, and who was a man of admirable wit, great ingenuity and learning, all which he had infused into his young pupil. This Frenchman was banished out of his own country for some heretical notions he held; and though he was a man of very little religion, he had admirable morals and a brave soul.

After the total defeat of Jamoan's army, which all fled or were left dead upon the place, they spent some time in the camp; Oroonoko choosing rather to remain a while there in his tents, than to enter into a p[a]lace, or live in a court where he had so lately suffered so great a loss. The officers therefore, who saw and knew his cause of discontent, invented all sorts of diversions and sports to entertain their prince; so that what with those amusements abroad and others at home, that is, within their tents, with the persuasions, arguments and care of his friends and servants that he more peculiarly prized, he wore off in time a great part of that chagrin and torture of despair which the first effects[54] of Imoinda's death had given him; insomuch as having received a thousand kind embassies from the king, and invitations to return to court, he obeyed, though with no little reluctance, and when he did so, there was a visible change in him, and for a long time he was much more melancholy than before. But time lessens all extremes, and reduces them to mediums[55] and unconcern; but no motives or beauties, though all endeavoured it, could engage him in any sort of amour, though he had all the invitations to it, both from his own youth and others' ambitions and designs.

Oroonoko was no sooner returned from this last conquest, and received at court with all the joy and magnificence that could be expressed to a young victor who was not only returned triumphant but beloved like a deity, than there arrived in the port an English ship.

This person[56] had often before been in these countries, and was very well known to Oroonoko, with whom he had trafficked for slaves, and had used to do the same with his predecessors.

This commander was a man of a finer sort of address and conversation, better bred and more engaging than most of that sort of men are; so that he seemed rather never to have been bred out of a court than almost all his life at sea. This captain therefore was always better received at court than most of the traders to those countries were; and especially by Oroonoko, who was more civilized, according to the European mode, than any other had been, and took more delight in the white nations, and, above all, men of parts and wit. To this captain he sold abundance of his slaves, and for the favour and esteem he had for him, made him many presents, and obliged him to stay at court as long as possibly he could. Which the captain seemed to take as a very great honour done him, entertaining the prince every day with globes and maps, and mathematical discourses and instruments; eating, drinking, hunting and living with him with so much familiarity that it was not to be doubted but he had gained very greatly upon the heart of this gallant young man. And the captain, in return of all these mighty favours, besought the prince to honour his vessel with his presence, some day or other, to dinner, before he should set sail; which he condescended to accept, and appointed his day. The captain, on his part, failed not to have all things in a readiness, in the most magnificent order he could possibly. And the day being come, the captain, in his boat, richly adorned with carpets and velvet cushions, rowed to the shore to receive the prince, with another long-boat, where was placed all his music and trumpets, with which Oroonoko was extremely delighted, who met him on the shore, attended by his French governor, Jamoan, Aboan and about an hundred of the noblest of the youths of the court. And after they had first carried the prince on board, the boats fetched the rest off, where they found a very splendid treat, with all sorts of fine wines, and were as well entertained as it was possible in such a place to be.

The prince having drunk hard of punch, and several sorts of wine, as did all the rest (for great care was taken they should want nothing of that part of the entertainment), was very merry, and in great admiration of the ship, for he had never been in one before, so that he was curious of beholding every place where he decently might descend. The rest, no less curious, who were not quite overcome with drinking, rambled at their pleasure fore and aft, as their fancies guided them; so that the captain, who had well laid his design before, gave the word and seized on all his guests, they clapping great irons suddenly on the prince when he was leaped down in the hold to view that part of the vessel, and locking him fast down, secured him. The same treachery was used to all the rest; and all in one instant, in several places of the ship, were lashed fast in irons and betrayed to slavery.[57] That great design over, they set all hands to work to hoist sail; and with as treacherous and fair a wind they made from the shore with this innocent and glorious prize, who thought of nothing less than such an entertainment.

Some have commended this act as brave in the captain; but I will spare my sense of it, and leave it to my reader to judge as he pleases.

It may be easily guessed in what manner the prince resented this indignity, who may be best resembled to a lion taken in a toil; so he raged, so he struggled for liberty, but all in vain; and they had so wisely managed his fetters that he could not use a hand in his defence to quit himself of a life that would by no means endure slavery, nor could he move from the place where he was tied to any solid part of the ship against which he might have beat his head and have finished his disgrace that way; so that being deprived of all other means, he resolved to perish for want of food. And pleased at last with that thought, and toiled and tired by rage and indignation, he laid himself down, and sullenly resolved upon dying, and refused all things that were brought him.

This did not a little vex the captain, and the more so because he found almost all of them of the same humour; so that the loss of so many brave slaves, so tall and goodly to behold, would have been very considerable. He therefore ordered one to go from him (for he would not be seen himself) to Oroonoko, and to assure him he was afflicted for having rashly done so inhospitable a deed, and which could not be now remedied, since they were far from shore; but since he resented it in so high a nature, he assured him, he would revoke his resolution, and set both him and his friends ashore on the next land they should touch at; and of this the messenger gave him his oath, provided he would resolve to live. And Oroonoko, whose honour was such as he never had violated a word in his life himself, much less a solemn asseveration, believed in an instant what this man said, but replied, he expected for a confirmation of this to have his shameful fetters dismissed. This demand was carried to the captain, who returned him answer that the offence had been so great which he had put upon the prince, that he durst not trust him with liberty while he remained in the ship, for fear lest by a valour natural to him, and a revenge that would animate that valour, he might commit some outrage fatal to himself and the king his master, to whom his vessel did belong.

To this Oroonoko replied, he would engage his honour to behave himself in all friendly order and manner, and obey the command of the captain, as he was lord of the king's vessel and general of those men under his command.

This was delivered to the still doubting captain, who could not resolve to trust a heathen he said, upon his parole,[58] a man that had no sense or notion of the God that he worshipped. Oroonoko then replied, he was very sorry to hear that the captain pretended to the knowledge and worship of any gods who had taught him no better principles than not to credit as he would be credited; but they told him the difference of their faith occasioned that distrust, for the captain had protested to him upon the word of a Christian, and sworn in the name of a great god, which if he should violate, he would expect eternal torment in the world to come. *Is that all the obligation he has to be just to his oath?* replied Oroonoko. *Let him know, I swear by my honour, which to violate, would not only render me contemptible and despised by all brave and honest men, and so give myself perpetual pain, but it would be eternally offending and diseasing all mankind, harming, betraying, circumventing and outraging all men; but punishments hereafter are suffered by oneself, and the world takes no cognizances whether this god have revenged them or not, it is done so secretly and deferred so long; while the man of no honour suffers every moment the scorn and contempt of the honester world, and dies every day ignominiously in his fame, which is more valuable than life. I speak not this to move belief, but to show you how you mistake, when you imagine that he who will violate his honour will keep his word with his gods.* So turning from him with a disdainful smile, he refused to answer him when he urged him to know what answer he should carry back to his captain, so that he departed without saying any more.

The captain pondering and consulting what to do, it was concluded that nothing but Oroonoko's liberty would encourage any of the rest to eat, except the Frenchman, whom the captain could not pretend to keep prisoner, but only told him, he was secured because he might act something in favour of the prince, but that he should be freed as soon as they came to land.

So that they concluded it wholly necessary to free the prince
from his irons, that he might show himself to the rest, that they
might have an eye upon him, and that they could not fear a
single man.

This being resolved, to make the obligation the greater, the
captain himself went to Oroonoko; where, after many compliments and assurances of what he had already promised, he
receiving from the prince his parole and his hand for his good
behaviour, dismissed his irons, and brought him to his own
cabin; where, after having treated and reposed him a while, for
he had neither eaten nor slept in four days before, he besought
him to visit those obstinate people in chains who refused all
manner of sustenance, and entreated him to oblige them to eat,
and assure them of their liberty the first opportunity.

Oroonoko, who was too generous not[59] to give credit to his
words, showed himself to his people, who were transported
with excess of joy at the sight of their darling prince; falling at
his feet, and kissing and embracing them, believing, as some
divine oracle, all he assured them. But he besought them to bear
their chains with that bravery that became those whom he had
seen act so nobly in arms; and that they could not give him
greater proofs of their love and friendship, since it was all the
security the captain (his friend) could have against the revenge,
he said, they might possibly justly take for the injuries sustained
by him. And they all with one accord assured him, they could
not suffer enough when it was for his repose and safety.

After this they no longer refused to eat, but took what was
brought them and were pleased with their captivity, since by it
they hoped to redeem the prince, who, all the rest of the voyage,
was treated with all the respect due to his birth; though nothing
could divert his melancholy, and he would often sigh for
Imoinda, and think this a punishment due to his misfortune in
having left that noble maid behind him that fatal night in the
otan, when he fled to the camp.

Possessed with a thousand thoughts of past joys with this fair
young person, and a thousand griefs for her eternal loss, he
endured a tedious voyage, and at last arrived at the mouth of
the river of Surinam, a colony belonging to the King of England,

and where they were to deliver some part of their slaves. There the merchants and gentlemen of the country going on board to demand those lots of slaves they had already agreed on, and amongst those the overseers of those plantations where I then chanced to be; the captain, who had given the word, ordered his men to bring up those noble slaves in fetters, whom I have spoken of, and having put them, some in one, and some in other lots, with women and children (which they call *pickaninnies*[60]), they sold them off as slaves to several merchants and gentlemen; not putting any two in one lot, because they would separate them far from each other, not daring to trust them together, lest rage and courage should put them upon contriving some great action to the ruin of the colony.

Oroonoko was first seized on and sold to our overseer, who had the first lot, with seventeen more of all sorts and sizes, but not one of quality with him. When he saw this, he found what they meant, for, as I said, he understood English pretty well; and being wholly unarmed and defenceless, so as it was in vain to make any resistance, he only beheld the captain with a look all fierce and disdainful, upbraiding him with eyes, that forced blushes on his guilty cheeks; he only cried in passing over the side of the ship, *Farewell, Sir! It is worth my suffering to gain so true a knowledge both of you and of your gods*[61] *by whom you swear*. And desiring those that held him to forbear their pains, and telling them he would make no resistance, he cried, *Come, my fellow-slaves, let us descend and see if we can meet with more honour and honesty in the next world we shall touch upon*. So he nimbly leapt into the boat, and showing no more concern, suffered himself to be rowed up the river with his seventeen companions.

The gentleman that bought him was a young Cornish gentleman, whose name was Trefry; a man of great wit and fine learning, and was carried into those parts by the Lord —[62] Governor, to manage all his affairs. He reflecting on the last words of Oroonoko to the captain, and beholding the richness of his vest,[63] no sooner came into the boat, but he fixed his eyes on him; and finding something so extraordinary in his face, his shape and mien, a greatness of look, and haughtiness in his air, and finding he spoke English, had a great mind to be enquiring into his quality and fortune; which, though Oroonoko endeavoured to hide by only confessing he was above the rank of common slaves, Trefry soon found he was yet something greater than he confessed; and from that moment began to conceive so vast an esteem for him that he ever after loved him as his dearest brother, and showed him all the civilities due to so great a man.

Trefry was a very good mathematician and a linguist, could speak French and Spanish; and in the three days they remained in the boat (for so long were they going from the ship to the plantation), he entertained Oroonoko so agreeably with his art and discourse that he was no less pleased with Trefry, than he was with the prince; and he thought himself at least fortunate in this, that since he was a slave, as long as he would suffer himself to remain so, he had a man of so excellent wit and parts for a master. So that before they had finished their voyage up the river, he made no scruple of declaring to Trefry all his fortunes, and most part of what I have here related, and put himself wholly into the hands of his new friend, whom he found resenting all the injuries were done him, and was charmed with all the greatnesses of his actions, which were recited with that modesty and delicate sense as wholly vanquished him, and subdued him to his interest. And he promised him on his word and honour, he would find the means to reconduct him to his own country again; assuring him he had a perfect abhorrence of so dishonourable an action, and that he would sooner have died, than have been the author of such a perfidy. He found the prince was very much concerned to know what became of his friends, and how they took their slavery; and Trefry promised to take care about the enquiring after their condition, and that he should have an account of them.

Though, as Oroonoko afterwards said, he had little reason to credit the words of a *backearay*,[64] yet he knew not why, but he saw a kind of sincerity and awful truth in the face of Trefry; he saw an honesty in his eyes, and he found him wise and witty enough to understand honour, for it was one of his maxims, *A man of wit could not be a knave or villain.*

In their passage up the river[65] they put in at several houses for

refreshment, and ever when they landed, numbers of people
would flock to behold this man; not but their eyes were daily
entertained with the sight of slaves, but the fame of Oroonoko
was gone before him, and all people were in admiration of his
beauty. Besides, he had a rich habit on, in which he was taken,
so different from the rest, and which the captain could not strip
him of because he was forced to surprise his person in the minute
he sold him. When he found his habit made him liable, as he
thought, to be gazed at the more, he begged Trefry to give him
something more befitting a slave, which he did, and took off his
robes. Nevertheless, he shone through all and his osenbrigs (a
sort of brown holland[66] suit he had on) could not conceal the
graces of his looks and mien; and he had no less admirers than
when he had his dazzling habit on. The royal youth appeared
in spite of the slave, and people could not help treating him
after a different manner without designing it; as soon as they
approached him, they venerated and esteemed him; his eyes
insensibly commanded respect, and his behaviour insinuated it
into every soul. So that there was nothing talked of but this
young and gallant slave, even by those who yet knew not that
he was a prince.

I ought to tell you that the Christians never buy any slaves
but they give them some name of their own,[67] their native ones
being likely very barbarous and hard to pronounce; so that Mr
Trefry gave Oroonoko that of Caesar, which name will live in
that country as long as that (scarce more) glorious one of the
great Roman, for it is most evident he wanted[68] no part of the
personal courage of that Caesar, and acted things as memorable,
had they been done in some part of the world replenished with
people and historians that might have given him his due. But his
misfortune was to fall in an obscure world that afforded only a
female pen to celebrate his fame,[69] though I doubt not but it had
lived from others' endeavours, if the Dutch, who immediately
after his time, took that country, had not killed, banished and
dispersed all those that were capable of giving the world this
great man's life, much better than I have done. And Mr Trefry,
who designed it, died before he began it, and bemoaned himself
for not having undertook it in time.[70]

For the future therefore, I must call Oroonoko, Caesar, since by that name only he was known in our western world, and by that name he was received on shore at Parham-House,[71] where he was destined a slave. But if the king himself (God bless him) had come ashore, there could not have been greater expectations by all the whole plantation, and those neighbouring ones, than was on ours at that time; and he was received more like a governor than a slave. Notwithstanding, as the custom was, they assigned him his portion of land, his house and his business, up in the plantation. But as it was more for form than any design to put him to his task, he endured no more of the slave but the name, and remained some days in the house, receiving all visits that were made him, without stirring towards that part of the plantation where the Negroes were.

At last, he would needs go view his land, his house and the business assigned him. But he no sooner came to the houses of the slaves, which are like a little town by itself, the Negroes all having left work, but they all came forth to behold him, and found he was that prince who had, at several times, sold most of them to these parts; and, from a veneration they pay to great men, especially if they know them, and from the surprise and awe they had at the sight of him, they all cast themselves at his feet, crying out in their language, *Live, O King! Long live, O King!* And kissing his feet, paid him even divine homage.

Several English gentlemen were with him; and what Mr Trefry had told them was here confirmed of which he himself before had no other witness than Caesar himself. But he was infinitely glad to find his grandeur confirmed by the adoration of all the slaves.

Caesar, troubled with their over-joy and over-ceremony, besought them to rise, and to receive him as their fellow-slave, assuring them he was no better. At which they set up with one accord a most terrible and hideous mourning and condoling, which he and the English had much ado to appease. But at last they prevailed with them, and they prepared all their barbarous music, and everyone killed and dressed something of his own stock (for every family has their land apart, on which, at their leisure-times, they breed all eatable things) and, clubbing it together, made a most magnificent supper, inviting their grandee[72] captain, their prince, to honour it with his presence, which he did, and several English with him, where they all waited on him, some playing, others dancing before him all the time, according to the manners of their several nations, and with unwearied industry, endeavouring to please and delight him.

While they sat at meat Mr Trefry told Caesar, that most of these young slaves were undone in love with a fine she-slave whom they had had about six months on their land. The prince, who never heard the name of love without a sigh, nor any mention of it without the curiosity of examining further into that tale, which of all discourses was most agreeable to him, asked, how they came to be so unhappy as to be all undone for one fair slave? Trefry, who was naturally amorous, and loved to talk of love as well as anybody, proceeded to tell him, they had the most charming black that ever was beheld on their plantation, about fifteen or sixteen years old, as he guessed; that, for his part, he had done nothing but sigh for her ever since she came, and that all the white beauties he had seen, never charmed him so absolutely as this fine creature had done; and that no man of any nation ever beheld her that did not fall in love with her, and that she had all the slaves perpetually at her feet, and the whole country resounded with the fame of Clemene,[73] *for so*, said he, *we have christened her. But she denies us all with such a noble disdain, that it is a miracle to see that she, who can give such eternal desires, should herself be all ice and unconcern. She is adorned with the most graceful modesty that ever beautified youth; the softest sigher – that, if she were capable of love, one would swear she languished for some absent happy man; and so retired, as if she feared a rape even from the God of Day,[74] or that the breezes would steal kisses from her delicate mouth. Her task of work some sighing lover every day makes it his petition to perform for her, which she accepts blushing, and with reluctance, for fear he will ask her a look for a recompense, which he dares not presume to hope, so great an awe she strikes into the hearts of her admirers. I do not wonder*, replied the prince, *that Clemene should refuse slaves, being as you say so beautiful, but wonder how she escapes those who*

*can entertain her as you can do. Or why, being your slave, you
do not oblige her to yield. I confess*, said Trefry, *when I have,
against her will, entertained her with love so long as to be
transported with my passion, even above decency, I have been
ready to make use of those advantages of strength and force
Nature has given me. But oh! she disarms me with that modesty
and weeping so tender and so moving that I retire, and thank
my stars she overcame me.* The company laughed at his civility
to a slave, and Caesar only applauded the nobleness of his
passion and nature, since that slave might be noble, or, what
was better, have true notions of honour and virtue in her.[75] Thus
passed they this night, after having received, from the slaves, all
imaginable respect and obedience.

The next day Trefry asked Caesar to walk when the heat was
allayed, and designedly carried him by the cottage of the fair
slave, and told him, she whom he spoke of last night lived there
retired. *But*, says he, *I would not wish you to approach, for I
am sure you will be in love as soon as you behold her.* Caesar
assured him, he was proof against all the charms of that sex,
and that if he imagined his heart could be so perfidious to love
again after Imoinda, he believed he should tear it from his
bosom. They had no sooner spoke, but a little shock-dog[76] that
Clemene had presented her, which she took great delight in, ran
out, and she, not knowing anybody was there, ran to get it in
again, and bolted out on those who were just speaking of her.
When seeing them, she would have run in again, but Trefry
caught her by the hand and cried, *Clemene, however you fly a
lover, you ought to pay some respect to this stranger* (pointing
to Caesar). But she, as if she had resolved never to raise her eyes
to the face of a man again, bent them the more to the earth
when he spoke, and gave the prince the leisure to look the
more at her. There needed no long gazing, or consideration, to
examine who this fair creature was. He soon saw Imoinda all
over her; in a minute he saw her face, her shape, her air, her
modesty, and all that called forth his soul with joy at his eyes,
and left his body destitute of almost life. It stood without
motion, and, for a minute, knew not that it had a being. And, I
believe, he had never come to himself, so oppressed he was with

over-joy, if he had not met with this allay,[77] that he perceived Imoinda fall dead in the hands of Trefry. This awakened him, and he ran to her aid, and caught her in his arms, where, by degrees, she came to herself; and it is needless to tell with what transports, what ecstasies of joy, they both a while beheld each other, without speaking, then snatched each other to their arms, then gazed again, as if they still doubted whether they possessed the blessing they grasped. But when they recovered their speech, it is not to be imagined what tender things they expressed to each other; wondering what strange fate had brought them again together. They soon informed each other of their fortunes, and equally bewailed their fate; but at the same time, they mutually protested, that even fetters and slavery were soft and easy, and would be supported with joy and pleasure while they could be so happy to possess each other, and be able to make good their vows. Caesar swore he disdained the empire of the world while he could behold his Imoinda and she despised grandeur and pomp, those vanities of her sex, when she could gaze on Oroonoko. He adored the very cottage where she resided, and said, that little inch of the world would give him more happiness than all the universe could do, and she vowed, it was a palace while adorned with the presence of Oroonoko.

Trefry was infinitely pleased with this novel,[78] and found this Clemene was the fair mistress of whom Caesar had before spoke; and was not a little satisfied that Heaven was so kind to the prince as to sweeten his misfortunes by so lucky an accident, and leaving the lovers to themselves, was impatient to come down to Parham-House (which was on the same plantation) to give me an account of what had happened. I was as impatient to make these lovers a visit, having already made a friendship with Caesar, and from his own mouth learned what I have related, which was confirmed by his Frenchman, who was set on shore to seek his fortune, and of whom they could not make a slave, because a Christian, and he came daily to Parham Hill to see and pay his respects to his pupil prince. So that concerning and interesting myself in all that related to Caesar, whom I had assured of liberty as soon as the governor arrived, I hasted presently to the place where these lovers were, and was infinitely glad to find this beautiful young slave (who had already gained all our esteems for her modesty and her extraordinary prettiness) to be the same I had heard Caesar speak so much of. One may imagine then, we paid her a treble respect; and though from her being carved in fine flowers and birds all over her body, we took her to be of quality before, yet, when we knew Clemene was Imoinda, we could not enough admire her.

I had forgot to tell you that those who are nobly born of that country are so delicately cut and raced[79] all over the fore part of the trunk of their bodies that it looks as if it were japanned; the works being raised like high point round the edges of the flowers.[80] Some are only carved with a little flower or bird at the sides of the temples, as was Caesar; and those who are so carved over the body resemble our ancient Picts[81] that are figured in the chronicles, but these carvings are more delicate.

From that happy day Caesar took Clemene for his wife, to the general joy of all people; and there was as much magnificence as the country would afford at the celebration of this wedding. And in a very short time after she conceived with child, which made Caesar even adore her, knowing he was the last of his great race. This new accident made him more impatient of liberty, and he was every day treating with Trefry for his and Clemene's liberty; and offered either gold, or a vast quantity of slaves, which should be paid before they let him go, provided he could have any security that he should go when his ransom was paid. They fed him from day to day with promises, and delayed him till the Lord Governor should come, so that he began to suspect them of falsehood, and that they would delay him till the time of his wife's delivery, and make a slave of that too, for all the breed is theirs to whom the parents belong.[82] This thought made him very uneasy, and his sullenness gave them some jealousies[83] of him, so that I was obliged, by some persons who feared a mutiny[84] (which is very fatal sometimes in those colonies that abound so with slaves that they exceed the whites in vast numbers), to discourse with Caesar, and to give him all the satisfaction I possibly could. They knew he and Clemene were scarce an hour in a day from my lodgings, that they ate with me, and that I obliged them in all things I was capable of: I entertained him with the lives of the Romans,[85] and great men, which charmed him to my company, and her with teaching her all the pretty works[86] that I was mistress of, and telling her stories of nuns,[87] and endeavouring to bring her to the knowledge of the true God. But of all discourses Caesar liked that the worst, and would never be reconciled to our notions of the Trinity, of which he ever made a jest; it was a riddle, he said, would turn his brain to conceive, and one could not make him understand what faith was. However, these conversations failed not altogether so well to divert him, that he liked the company of us women much above the men, for he could not drink, and he is but an ill companion in that country that cannot. So that obliging him to love us very well, we had all the liberty of speech with him, especially myself, whom he called his Great Mistress; and indeed my word would go a great way with him. For these reasons, I had opportunity to take notice to him that he was not well pleased of late, as he used to be, was more retired and thoughtful, and told him, I took it ill he should suspect we would break our words with him, and not permit both him and Clemene to return to his own kingdom, which was not so long away but when he was once on his voyage he would quickly arrive there. He made me some answers that showed a doubt in him, which made me ask him, what advantage it would be to doubt? It would but give us a fear of him, and possibly compel us to treat him so as I should be very loth to behold; that is, it might occasion his confinement. Perhaps this was not so luckily spoke of me, for I perceived he resented that word, which I strove to soften again in vain. However, he assured me, that whatsoever resolutions he should take, he would act nothing upon the white people; and as for myself, and those upon that plantation where he was, he would sooner forfeit his eternal liberty, and life itself, than lift his hand against his greatest enemy on that place. He besought me to suffer no fears upon his account, for he could do nothing that honour should not dictate, but he accused himself for having suffered slavery so long; yet he charged that weakness on love alone, who was capable of making him neglect even glory itself, and, for which, now he reproaches himself every moment of the day. Much more to this effect he spoke, with an air impatient enough to make me know he would not be long in bondage, and though he suffered only the name of a slave, and had nothing of the toil and labour of one, yet that was sufficient to render him uneasy, and he had been too long idle who used to be always in action and in arms. He had a spirit all rough and fierce, and that could not be tamed to lazy rest, and though all endeavours were used to exercise himself in such actions and sports as this world afforded, as running, wrestling, pitching the bar,[88] hunting and fishing, chasing and killing tigers[89] of a monstrous size, which this continent affords in abundance, and wonderful snakes, such as Alexander is reported to have encountered at the river of Amazons,[90] and which Caesar took great delight to overcome; yet these were not actions great enough for his large soul, which was still panting after more renowned action.

Before I parted that day with him, I got, with much ado, a promise from him to rest yet a little longer with patience, and wait the coming of the Lord Governor, who was every day expected on our shore. He assured me, he would, and this promise he desired me to know was given perfectly in complaisance to me, in whom he had an entire confidence.

After this, I neither thought it convenient to trust him much out of our view, nor did the country who feared him; but with one accord it was advised to treat him fairly, and oblige him to remain within such a compass, and that he should be permitted, as seldom as could be, to go up to the plantations of the Negroes; or, if he did, to be accompanied by some that should be rather in appearance attendants than spies. This care was for some time taken, and Caesar looked upon it as a mark of extraordinary respect, and was glad his discontent had obliged them to be more observant to him. He received new assurance from the overseer, which was confirmed to him by the opinion of all the gentlemen of the country who made their court to him. During this time that we had his company more frequently than hitherto we had had, it may not be unpleasant to relate to you the diversions we entertained him with, or rather he us.

My stay was to be short in that country, because my father

died at sea,[91] and never arrived to possess the honour designed
him (which was lieutenant-general[92] of six and thirty islands,
besides the continent[93] of Surinam), nor the advantages he hoped
to reap by them, so that though we were obliged to continue on
our voyage, we did not intend to stay upon the place. Though,
in a word, I must say thus much of it, that certainly had his late
Majesty,[94] of sacred memory, but seen and known what a vast
and charming world he had been master of in that continent, he
would never have parted so easily with it to the Dutch.[95] It is a
continent whose vast extent was never yet known, and may
contain more noble earth than all the universe besides; for, they
say, it reaches from east to west, one way as far as China, and
another to Peru. It affords all things both for beauty and use; it
is there eternal Spring, always the very months of April, May
and June. The shades are perpetual, the trees, bearing at once
all degrees of leaves and fruit, from blooming buds to ripe
Autumn,[96] groves of oranges, lemons, citrons, figs, nutmegs and
noble aromatics, continually bearing their fragrancies. The trees
appearing all like nosegays adorned with flowers of different
kind; some are all white, some purple, some scarlet, some blue,
some yellow; bearing, at the same time, ripe fruit and blooming
young or producing every day new. The very wood of all these
trees have an intrinsic value above common timber, for they are,
when cut, of different colours, glorious to behold, and bear a
price considerable, to inlay withal. Besides this, they yield rich
balm and gums, so that we make our candles of such an aromatic
substance as does not only give a sufficient light, but, as they
burn, they cast their perfumes all about. Cedar is the common
firing, and all the houses are built with it. The very meat we eat,
when set on the table, if it be native, I mean of the country,
perfumes the whole room, especially a little beast called an
armadillo, a thing which I can liken to nothing so well as a
rhinoceros: it is all in white armour, so jointed that it moves as
well in it as if it had nothing on. This beast is about the bigness
of a pig of six weeks old.[97] But it were endless to give an account
of all the divers wonderful and strange things that country
affords, and which we took a very great delight to go in search
of, though those adventures are oftentimes fatal and at least

dangerous. But while we had Caesar in our company on these designs we feared no harm, nor suffered any.

As soon as I came into the country, the best house in it was presented me, called St John's Hill.[98] It stood on a vast rock of white marble, at the foot of which the river ran a vast depth down, and not to be descended on that side. The little waves still dashing and washing the foot of this rock made the softest murmurs and purlings in the world, and the opposite bank was adorned with such vast quantities of different flowers eternally blowing[99] and every day and hour new, fenced behind them with lofty trees of a thousand rare forms and colours, that the prospect was the most ravishing that sands[100] can create. On the edge of this white rock, towards the river, was a walk or grove of orange and lemon trees, about half the length of the Mall[101] here, whose flowery and fruity branches meet[102] at the top and hindered the sun, whose rays are very fierce there, from entering a beam into the grove, and the cool air that came from the river made it not only fit to entertain people in, at all the hottest hours of the day, but refreshed the sweet blossoms, and made it always sweet and charming, and sure the whole globe of the world cannot show so delightful a place as this grove was. Not all the gardens of boasted Italy can produce a shade to out-vie this which Nature had joined with Art to render so exceeding fine. And it is a marvel to see how such vast trees, as big as English oaks, could take footing on so solid a rock and in so little earth as covered that rock, but all things by Nature there are rare, delightful and wonderful. But to our sports.

Sometimes we would go surprising, and in search of young tigers in their dens, watching when the old ones went forth to forage for prey, and oftentimes we have been in great danger and have fled apace for our lives when surprised by the dams. But once, above all other times, we went on this design, and Caesar was with us, who had no sooner stolen a young tiger from her nest, but going off, we encountered the dam, bearing a buttock of a cow, which he[103] had torn off with his mighty paw, and going with it towards his den. We had only four women, Caesar and an English gentleman, brother to Harry Martin, the great Oliverian.[104] We found there was no escaping this enraged and ravenous beast. However, we women fled as fast as we could from it, but our heels had not saved our lives if Caesar had not laid down his cub when he found the tiger quit her prey to make more speed towards him, and taking Mr Martin's sword, desired him to stand aside or follow the ladies. He obeyed him, and Caesar met this monstrous beast of might, size and vast limbs, who came with open jaws upon him, and fixing his awful stern eyes full upon those of the beast and putting himself into a very steady and good aiming posture of defence, ran his sword quite through his breast, down to his very heart, home to the hilt of the sword. The dying beast stretched forth her paw, and going to grasp his thigh, surprised with death in that very moment, did him no other harm than fixing her long nails in his flesh very deep, feebly wounded him, but could not grasp the flesh to tear off any. When he had done this, he hollowed to us to return, which, after some assurance of his victory, we did, and found him lugging out the sword from the bosom of the tiger, who was laid in her blood on the ground. He took up the cub, and with an unconcern that had nothing of the joy or gladness of a victory, he came and laid the whelp at my feet. We all extremely wondered at his daring, and at the bigness of the beast, which was about the height of an heifer, but of mighty, great and strong limbs.

Another time, being in the woods, he killed a tiger which had long infested that part, and borne away abundance of sheep and oxen and other things that were for the support of those to whom they belonged. Abundance of people assailed this beast, some affirming they had shot her with several bullets quite through the body at several times, and some swearing they shot her through the very heart, and they believed she was a devil rather than a mortal thing. Caesar had often said, he had a mind to encounter this monster, and spoke with several gentlemen who had attempted her, one crying, *I shot her with so many poisoned arrows*, another with his gun in this part of her, and another in that. So that he remarking all these places where she was shot, fancied still he should overcome her by giving her another sort of a wound than any had yet done, and one day said (at the table), *What trophies and garlands, ladies, will you*

make me, if I bring you home the heart of this ravenous beast
that eats up all your lambs and pigs? We all promised he should
be rewarded at all our hands. So taking a bow, which he chose
out of a great many, he went up in the wood, with two gentlemen, where he imagined this devourer to be. They had not
passed very far in it, but they heard her voice, growling and
grumbling, as if she were pleased with something she was doing.
When they came in view, they found her muzzling in the belly
of a new-ravished sheep, which she had torn open, and seeing
herself approached, she took fast hold of her prey with her
fore-paws, and set a very fierce raging look on Caesar, without
offering to approach him, for fear, at the same time, of losing
what she had in possession. So that Caesar remained a good
while only taking aim and getting an opportunity to shoot her
where he designed. It was some time before he could accomplish
it; and to wound her and not kill her would but have enraged
her more and endangered him. He had a quiver of arrows at his
side, so that if one failed he could be supplied. At last, retiring
a little, he gave her opportunity to eat, for he found she was
ravenous and fell to as soon as she saw him retire, being more
eager of her prey than of doing new mischiefs. When he going
softly to one side of her, and hiding his person behind certain
herbage that grew high and thick, he took so good aim that, as
he intended, he shot her just into the eye; and the arrow was
sent with so good a will and so sure a hand that it stuck in her
brain and made her caper and become mad for a moment or
two, but being seconded by another arrow, he fell dead upon
the prey. Caesar cut him open with a knife, to see where those
wounds were that had been reported to him, and why he did
not die of them. But I shall now relate a thing that possibly will
find no credit among men, because it is a notion commonly
received with us, that nothing can receive a wound in the heart
and live; but when the heart of this courageous animal was
taken out, there were seven bullets of lead in it, and the wounds
seamed up with great scars, and she lived with the bullets a great
while, for it was long since they were shot. This heart the
conqueror brought up to us,[105] and it was a very great curiosity

which all the country came to see, and which gave Caesar occasion of many fine discourses, of accidents in war and strange escapes.

At other times he would go a-fishing, and discoursing on that diversion, he found we had in that country a very strange fish, called a numb eel[106] (an eel of which I have eaten) that, while it is alive, it has a quality so cold that those who are angling, though with a line of never so great a length, with a rod at the end of it, it shall, in the same minute the bait is touched by this eel, seize him or her that holds the rod with benumbedness that shall deprive them of sense for a while. And some have fallen into the water, and others dropped as dead on the banks of the rivers where they stood as soon as this fish touches the bait. Caesar used to laugh at this, and believed it impossible a man could lose his force at the touch of a fish; and could not understand that philosophy,[107] that a cold quality should be of that nature. However, he had a great curiosity to try whether it would have the same effect on him it had on others, and often tried, but in vain. At last, the sought for fish came to the bait, as he stood angling on the bank; and instead of throwing away the rod, or giving it a sudden twitch out of the water, whereby he might have caught both the eel and have dismissed the rod before it could have too much power over him, for experiment sake he grasped it but the harder, and fainting fell into the river. And being still possessed of the rod, the tide carried him senseless as he was a great way, till an Indian boat took him up and perceived, when they touched him, a numbness seize them, and by that knew the rod was in his hand, which, with a paddle (that is, a short oar) they struck away, and snatched it into the boat, eel and all. If Caesar was almost dead with the effect of this fish, he was more so with that of the water where he had remained the space of going a league,[108] and they found they had much ado to bring him back to life. But, at last, they did, and brought him home, where he was in a few hours well recovered and refreshed; and not a little ashamed to find he should be overcome by an eel, and that all the people who heard his defiance would laugh at him. But we cheered him up, and he, being convinced, we had the eel at supper; which was a quarter of an ell about and most delicate meat; and was of the more value since it cost so dear as almost the life of so gallant a man.

About this time we were in many mortal fears about some disputes the English had with the Indians, so that we could scarce trust ourselves, without great numbers, to go to any Indian towns or place where they abode, for fear they should fall upon us, as they did immediately after my coming away, and that it was in the possession of the Dutch who used them not so civilly as the English, so that they cut in pieces all they could take, getting into houses and hanging up the mother and all her children about her; and cut a footman, I left behind me, all in joints, and nailed him to trees.[109]

This feud began while I was there, so that I lost half the satisfaction I proposed, in not seeing and visiting the Indian towns. But one day, bemoaning of our misfortunes upon this account, Caesar told us, we need not fear, for if we had a mind to go, he would undertake to be our guard. Some would, but most would not venture. About eighteen of us resolved and took barge, and, after eight days, arrived near an Indian town. But approaching it, the hearts of some of our company failed and they would not venture on shore, so we polled who would and who would not. For my part, I said, if Caesar would, I would go. He resolved, so did my brother, and my woman, a maid of good courage. Now none of us speaking the language of the people, and imagining we should have a half diversion in gazing only and not knowing what they said, we took a fisherman that lived at the mouth of the river, who had been a long inhabitant there, and obliged him to go with us. But because he was known to the Indians, as trading among them and being, by long living there, become a perfect Indian in colour, we, who resolved to surprise them by making them see something they never had seen (that is, white people), resolved only myself, my brother and woman should go. So Caesar, the fisherman and the rest, hiding behind some thick reeds and flowers that grew in the banks, let us pass on towards the town which was on the bank of the river all along. A little distant from the houses, or huts, we saw some dancing, others busied in fetching and carrying of water from the river. They had no sooner spied us, but they set up a loud cry that frighted us at first. We thought it had been for those that should kill us, but it seems it was of wonder and amazement. They were all naked, and we were dressed so as is most commode[110] for the hot countries, very glittering and rich, so that we appeared extremely fine. My own hair was cut short, and I had a taffeta cap with black feathers on my head.[111] My brother was in a stuff[112] suit with silver loops and buttons, and abundance of green ribbon. This was all infinitely surprising to them, and because we saw them stand still till we approached them, we took heart and advanced, came up to them and offered them our hands, which they took, and looked on us round about, calling still for more company, who came swarming out, all wondering and crying out *tepeeme*,[113] taking their hair up in their hands, and spreading it wide to those they called out to, as if they would say (as indeed it signified), *numberless wonders*, or not to be recounted, no more than to number the hair of their heads. By degrees they grew more bold, and from gazing upon us round, they touched us, laying their hands upon all the features of our faces, feeling our breasts and arms, taking up one petticoat, then wondering to see another, admiring our shoes and stockings, but more our garters, which we gave them, and they tied about their legs, being laced with silver lace at the ends, for they much esteem any shining things. In fine, we suffered them to survey us as they pleased, and we thought they would never have done admiring us. When Caesar and the rest saw we were received with such wonder, they came up to us, and finding the Indian trader whom they knew (for it is by these fishermen, called Indian traders, we hold a commerce with them; for they love not to go far from home, and we never go to them), when they saw him therefore, they set up a new joy, and cried in their language, *Oh! here's our tiguamy, and we shall now know whether those things can speak*. So advancing to him, some of them gave him their hands and cried, *Amora tiguamy*,[114] which is as much as, *How do you do*, or, *Welcome friend*, and all with one din began to gabble to him and asked, if we had sense and wit? If we could talk of affairs of life and war, as they could do? If we could hunt, swim and do a thousand things they

use? He answered them, we could. Then they invited us into
their houses, and dressed venison and buffalo for us; and, going
out, gathered a leaf of a tree, called a *sarumbo* leaf, of six yards
long, and spread it on the ground for a table-cloth,[115] and cutting
another in pieces instead of plates, setting us on little low Indian
stools, which they cut out of one entire piece of wood and paint
in a sort of japan-work. They serve every one their mess[116] on
these pieces of leaves, and it was very good, but too high-
seasoned with pepper. When we had eaten, my brother and I
took out our flutes and played to them, which gave them new
wonder; and I soon perceived, by an admiration that is natural
to these people, and by the extreme ignorance and simplicity
of them, it were not difficult to establish any unknown or
extravagant religion among them, and to impose any notions
or fictions upon them. For seeing a kinsman of mine set some
paper a-fire with a burning-glass, a trick they had never before
seen,[117] they were like to have adored him for a god, and begged
he would give them the characters or figures of his name that
they might oppose it against winds and storms, which he did,
and they held it up in those seasons and fancied it had a charm
to conquer them, and kept it like a holy relic. They are very
superstitious, and called him the great *peeie*,[118] that is, prophet.
They showed us their Indian *peeie*, a youth of about sixteen
years old, as handsome as Nature could make a man. They
consecrate a beautiful youth from his infancy, and all arts are
used to complete him in the finest manner, both in beauty and
shape. He is bred to all the little arts and cunning they are
capable of, to all the legerdemain tricks, and sleight of hand,
whereby he imposes upon the rabble, and is both a doctor in
physic and divinity. And by these tricks makes the sick believe
he sometimes eases their pains, by drawing from the afflicted
part little serpents, or odd flies, or worms, or any strange thing;
and though they have besides undoubted good remedies for
almost all their diseases, they cure the patient more by fancy
than by medicines, and make themselves feared, loved and
reverenced. This young *peeie* had a very young wife, who, seeing
my brother kiss her, came running and kissed me; after this,
they kissed one another, and made it a very great jest, it being

so novel, and new admiration and laughing went round the multitude that they never will forget that ceremony never before used or known. Caesar had a mind to see and talk with their war captains, and we were conducted to one of their houses, where we beheld several of the great captains who had been at council. But so frightful a vision it was to see them no fancy can create; no such dreams can represent so dreadful a spectacle. For my part I took them for hobgoblins, or fiends, rather than men. But however their shapes appeared, their souls were very humane and noble, but some wanted their noses, some their lips, some both noses and lips, some their ears, and others cut through each cheek, with long slashes, through which their teeth appeared; they had several other[119] formidable wounds and scars, or rather dismemberings. They had *comitias*[120] or little aprons before them, and girdles of cotton with their knives naked stuck in it, a bow at their backs, and a quiver of arrows on their thighs, and most had feathers on their heads of divers colours. They cried *Amora tiguamy* to us at our entrance, and were pleased we said as much to them. They seated us, and gave us drink of the best sort, and wondered, as much as the others had done before, to see us. Caesar was marvelling as much at their faces, wondering how they should all be so wounded in war; he was impatient to know how they all came by those frightful marks of rage or malice, rather than wounds got in noble battle. They told us by our interpreter, that when any war was waging, two men chosen out by some old captain, whose fighting was past and who could only teach the theory of war, these two men were to stand in competition for the generalship, or Great War Captain, and being brought before the old judges, now past labour, they are asked, what they dare do to show they are worthy to lead an army? When he, who is first asked making no reply, cuts off his nose and throws it contemptibly[121] on the ground, and the other does something to himself that he thinks surpasses him, and perhaps deprives himself of lips and an eye. So they slash on till one gives out, and many have died in this debate.[122] And it is by a passive valour they show and prove their activity, a sort of courage too brutal to be applauded by our black hero; nevertheless, he expressed his esteem of them.

In this voyage Caesar begot so good an understanding between the Indians and the English that there were no more fears or heartburnings[123] during our stay, but we had a perfect, open and free trade with them. Many things remarkable and worthy reciting we met with in this short voyage, because Caesar made it his business to search out and provide for our entertainment, especially to please his dearly adored Imoinda, who was a sharer in all our adventures; we being resolved to make her chains as easy as we could, and to compliment the prince in that manner that most obliged him.

As we were coming up again, we met with some Indians of strange aspects, that is, of a larger size and other sort of features than those of our country. Our Indian slaves that rowed us asked them some questions, but they could not understand us, but showed us a long cotton string with several knots on it,[124] and told us, they had been coming from the mountains so many moons[125] as there were knots. They were habited in skins of a strange beast, and brought along with them bags of gold dust,[126] which, as well as they could give us to understand, came streaming in little small channels down the high mountains when the rains fell; and offered to be the convoy to anybody, or persons, that would go to the mountains. We carried these men up to Parham, where they were kept till the Lord Governor came. And because all the country was mad to be going on this golden adventure, the governor by his letters commanded (for they sent some of the gold to him) that a guard should be set at the mouth of the River of Amazons[127] (a river so called, almost as broad as the river of Thames), and prohibited all people from going up that river, it conducting to those mountains of gold.[128] But we going off for England before the project was further prosecuted, and the governor being drowned in a hurricane,[129] either the design died or the Dutch have the advantage of it. And it is to be bemoaned what His Majesty lost by losing that part of America.[130]

Though this digression is a little from my story, however, since it contains some proofs of the curiosity and daring of this great man, I was content to omit nothing of his character.

It was thus for some time we diverted him. But now Imoinda

began to show she was with child, and did nothing but sigh and weep for the captivity of her lord, herself and the infant yet unborn, and believed, if it were so hard to gain the liberty of two, it would be more difficult to get that for three. Her griefs were so many darts in the great heart of Caesar, and taking his opportunity one Sunday, when all the whites were overtaken in drink, as there were abundance of several trades and slaves for four years[131] that inhabited among the Negro houses, and Sunday was their day of debauch (otherwise they were a sort of spies upon Caesar), he went pretending out of goodness to them to feast among them, and sent all his music, and ordered a great treat for the whole gang, about three hundred Negroes. And about a hundred and fifty were able to bear arms, such as they had, which were sufficient to do execution with spirits[132] accordingly. For the English had none but rusty swords that no strength could draw from a scabbard, except the people of particular quality, who took care to oil them and keep them in good order. The guns also, unless here and there one, or those newly carried from England, would do no good or harm, for it is the nature of that county[133] to rust and eat up iron or any metals but gold and silver. And they are very inexpert at the bow, which the Negroes and the Indians are perfect masters of.

Caesar, having singled out these men from the women and children, made a harangue to them of the miseries and ignominies of slavery; counting up all their toils and sufferings under such loads, burdens and drudgeries as were fitter for beasts than men; senseless brutes, than human souls. He told them, it was not for days, months or years, but for eternity; there was no end to be of their misfortunes. They suffered not like men who might find a glory and fortitude in oppression, but like dogs that loved the whip and bell,[134] and fawned the more they were beaten. That they had lost the divine quality of men and were become insensible asses, fit only to bear. Nay worse, an ass, or dog, or horse having done his duty, could lie down in retreat, and rise to work again, and while he did his duty, endured no stripes; but men, villainous, senseless men such as they, toiled on all the tedious week till black Friday,[135] and then, whether they worked or not, whether they were faulty or meriting, they promiscuously, the innocent with the guilty, suffered the infamous whip, the sordid stripes, from their fellow-slaves till their blood trickled from all parts of their body, blood whose every drop ought to be revenged with a life of some of those tyrants that impose it. *And why*, said he, *my dear friends and fellow-sufferers, should we be slaves to an unknown people? Have they vanquished us nobly in fight? Have they won us in honourable battle? And are we by the chance of war become their slaves? This would not anger a noble heart, this would not animate a soldier's soul. No, but we are bought and sold like apes or monkeys, to be the sport of women, fools and cowards, and the support of rogues, runagades*[136] *that have abandoned their own countries for raping, murders, theft and villainies. Do you not hear every day how they upbraid each other with infamy of life, below the wildest savages? And shall we render obedience to such a degenerate race, who have no one human virtue left to distinguish them from the vilest creatures? Will you, I say, suffer the lash from such hands?*[137] They all replied with one accord, *No, no, no; Caesar has spoke like a great captain, like a great king.*

After this he would have proceeded, but was interrupted by a tall Negro of some more quality than the rest. His name was Tuscan, who bowing at the feet of Caesar, cried, *My Lord, we have listened with joy and attention to what you have said, and, were we only men, would follow so great a leader through the world. But oh! consider, we are husbands and parents too, and have things more dear to us than life: our wives and children unfit for travel in those unpassable woods, mountains, and bogs. We have not only difficult lands to overcome, but rivers to wade and mountains to encounter; ravenous beasts of prey.* To this Caesar replied, that honour was the first principle in Nature that was to be obeyed; but as no man would pretend to that, without all the acts of virtue, compassion, charity, love, justice and reason, he found it not inconsistent with that to take equal care of their wives and children as they would of themselves; and that he did not design, when he led them to freedom and glorious liberty, that they should leave that better part of themselves to perish by the hand of the tyrant's whip. But if there were a woman among them so degenerate from love and virtue to choose slavery before the pursuit of her husband, and with the hazard of her life to share with him in his fortunes, that such an one ought to be abandoned and left as a prey to the common enemy.

To which they all agreed – and bowed. After this he spoke of the impassable woods and rivers, and convinced them, the more danger, the more glory. He told them, that he had heard of one Hannibal, a great captain, had cut his way through mountains of solid rocks,[138] and should a few shrubs oppose them which they could fire before them? No, it was a trifling excuse to men resolved to die or overcome. As for bogs, they are with a little labour filled and hardened, and the rivers could be no obstacle, since they swam by nature, at least by custom, from the first hour of their birth. That when the children were weary, they must carry them by turns, and the woods and their own industry would afford them food. To this they all assented with joy.

Tuscan then demanded, what he would do? He said, they would travel towards the sea, plant a new colony and defend it by their valour; and when they could find a ship, either driven by stress of weather or guided by providence that way, they would seize it, and make it a prize till it had transported them to their own countries. At least, they should be made free in his kingdom, and be esteemed as his fellow-sufferers, and men that had the courage and the bravery to attempt, at least, for liberty. And if they died in the attempt it would be more brave than to live in perpetual slavery.

They bowed and kissed his feet at this resolution, and with one accord vowed to follow him to death. And that night was appointed to begin their march; they made it known to their wives and directed them to tie their hamaca[139] about their shoulder, and under their arm, like a scarf, and to lead their children that could go, and carry those that could not. The wives who pay an entire obedience to their husbands obeyed, and stayed for them where they were appointed. The men stayed but to furnish themselves with what defensive arms they could get, and all met at the rendezvous where Caesar made a new encouraging speech to them, and led them out.

But as they could not march far that night, on Monday early, when the overseers went to call them all together to go to work, they were extremely surprised to find not one upon the place, but all fled with what baggage they had. You may imagine this news was not only suddenly spread all over the plantation, but soon reached the neighbouring ones, and we had by noon about six hundred men they call the militia of the country that came to assist us in the pursuit of the fugitives. But never did one see so comical an army march forth to war. The men of any fashion would not concern themselves, though it were almost the common cause, for such revoltings are very ill examples, and have very fatal consequences oftentimes in many colonies. But they had a respect for Caesar, and all hands were against the Parhamites, as they called those of Parham Plantation,[140] because they did not, in the first place, love the Lord Governor; and secondly, they would have it that Caesar was ill used and baffled with.[141] And it is not impossible but some of the best in the country was of his counsel in this flight and depriving us of all the slaves, so that they of the better sort would not meddle in the matter. The deputy governor,[142] of whom I have had no great occasion to speak, and who was the most fawning, fair-tongued fellow in the world and one that pretended the most friendship to Caesar, was now the only violent man against him, and though he had nothing and so need fear nothing, yet talked and looked bigger than any man. He was a fellow whose character is not fit to be mentioned with the worst of the slaves. This fellow would lead his army forth to meet Caesar, or rather to pursue him. Most of their arms were of those sort of cruel whips they call cat with nine tails;[143] some had rusty useless guns for show, others old basket-hilts[144] whose blades had never seen the light in this age, and others had long staffs and clubs. Mr Trefry went along, rather to be a mediator than a conqueror in such a battle; for he foresaw, and knew, if by fighting they put the Negroes into despair, they were a sort of sullen fellows that would drown or kill themselves before they would yield,[145] and he advised that fair means was best. But Byam was one that abounded his own wit,[146] and would take his own measures.

It was not hard to find these fugitives, for as they fled they were forced to fire and cut the woods before them, so that night or day they pursued them by the light they made, and by the path they had cleared. But as soon as Caesar found he was pursued, he put himself in a posture of defence, placing all the women and children in the rear, and himself, with Tuscan by his side, or next to him, all promising to die or conquer. Encouraged thus, they never stood to parley, but fell on pell-mell upon the English, and killed some, and wounded a good many, they having recourse to their whips as the best of their weapons. And as they observed no order, they perplexed the enemy so sorely with lashing them in the eyes. And the women and children, seeing their husbands so treated, being of fearful cowardly dispositions and hearing the English cry out, *Yield and live, yield and be pardoned*, they all run in amongst their husbands and fathers, and hung about them, crying out, *Yield, yield, and leave Caesar to their revenge*, that by degrees the slaves abandoned Caesar, and left him only Tuscan and his heroic Imoinda, who, grown big as she was, did nevertheless press near her lord, having a bow and a quiver full of poisoned arrows, which she managed with such dexterity that she wounded several and shot the governor into the shoulder; of which wound he had like to have died, but that an Indian woman, his mistress, sucked the wound and cleansed it from the venom. But however, he stirred not from the place till he had parlied with Caesar, who he found was resolved to die fighting, and would not be taken; no more would Tuscan or Imoinda. But he, more thirsting after revenge of another sort than that of depriving him of life, now made use of all his art of talking and dissembling, and besought Caesar to yield himself upon terms which he himself should propose and should be sacredly assented to and kept by him. He told him, it was not that he any longer feared him, or could believe the force of two men and a young heroine could overcome all them, and with all the slaves now on their side also; but it was the vast esteem he had for his person, the desire he had to serve so gallant a man, and to hinder himself from the reproach hereafter of having been the occasion of the death of a prince whose valour and magnanimity deserved the empire of the world. He protested to him, he looked upon this action as

gallant and brave, however tending to the prejudice of his lord
and master, who would by it have lost so considerable a number
of slaves; that this flight of his should be looked on as a heat
of youth, and a rashness of a too forward courage, and an
unconsidered impatience of liberty, and no more; and that he
laboured in vain to accomplish that which they would effectually
perform as soon as any ship arrived that would touch on his
coast. *So that if you will be pleased*, continued he, *to surrender
yourself, all imaginable respect shall be paid you; and yourself,
your wife, and child, if it be born here, shall depart free out of
our land.* But Caesar would hear of no composition,[147] though
Byam urged, if he pursued and went on in his design, he would
inevitably perish, either by great snakes, wild beasts or hunger,
and he ought to have regard to his wife, whose condition
required ease and not the fatigues of tedious travel, where she
could not be secured from being devoured. But Caesar told him,
there was no faith in the white men or the gods they adored who
instructed them in principles so false that honest men could not
live amongst them; though no people professed so much, none
performed so little; that he knew what he had to do when he
dealt with men of honour, but with them a man ought to be
eternally on his guard and never to eat and drink with Christians
without his weapon of defence in his hand, and, for his own
security, never to credit one word they spoke. As for the rashness
and inconsiderateness of his action, he would confess the governor is in the right, and that he was ashamed of what he had
done in endeavouring to make those free, who were by nature
slaves, poor wretched rogues fit to be used as Christians' tools;
dogs, treacherous and cowardly, fit for such masters, and they
wanted only but to be whipped into the knowledge of the
Christian gods to be the vilest of all creeping things, to learn to
worship such deities as had not power to make them just, brave
or honest.[148] In fine,[149] after a thousand things of this nature,
not fit here to be recited, he told Byam, he had rather die than
live upon the same earth with such dogs. But Trefry and Byam
pleaded and protested together so much that Trefry, believing
the governor to mean what he said, and speaking very cordially
himself, generously put himself into Caesar's hands, and took

him aside, and persuaded him, even with tears, to live by surrendering himself, and to name his conditions. Caesar was overcome by his wit and reasons, and, in consideration of Imoinda, and demanding what he desired, and that it should be ratified by their hands in writing because he had perceived that was the common way of contract between man and man amongst the whites. All this was performed, and Tuscan's pardon was put in, and they surrendered to the governor, who walked peaceably down into the plantation with them after giving order to bury their dead. Caesar was very much toiled with the bustle of the day, for he had fought like a Fury,[150] and what mischief was done, he and Tuscan performed alone, and gave their enemies a fatal proof that they durst do anything, and feared no mortal force.

But they were no sooner arrived at the place where all the slaves receive their punishments of whipping, but they laid hands on Caesar and Tuscan, faint with heat and toil; and surprising them, bound them to two several stakes, and whipped them in a most deplorable and inhumane manner, rending the very flesh from their bones; especially Caesar, who was not perceived to make any moan or to alter his face, only to roll his eyes on the faithless governor, and those he believed guilty, with fierceness and indignation. And, to complete his rage, he saw every one of those slaves, who, but a few days before, adored him as something more than mortal, now had a whip to give him some lashes,[151] while he strove not to break his fetters, though, if he had, it were impossible. But he pronounced a woe and revenge from his eyes that darted fire, which was at once both awful and terrible to behold.

When they thought they were sufficiently revenged on him, they untied him, almost fainting with loss of blood from a thousand wounds all over his body, from which they had rent his clothes, and led him bleeding and naked as he was, and loaded him all over with irons, and then rubbed his wounds, to complete their cruelty, with Indian pepper, which had like to have made him raving mad, and, in this condition made him so fast to the ground that he could not stir if his pains and wounds would have given him leave. They spared Imoinda, and did not let her see this barbarity committed towards her lord, but carried her down to Parham and shut her up, which was not in kindness to her, but for fear she should die with the sight or miscarry, and then they should lose a young slave, and perhaps the mother.

You must know, that when the news was brought on Monday morning, that Caesar had betaken himself to the woods and carried with him all the Negroes, we were possessed with extreme fear, which no persuasions could dissipate, that he would secure himself till night, and then, that he would come down and cut all our throats. This apprehension made all the females of us fly down the river to be secured, and while we were away, they acted this cruelty. For I suppose I had authority and interest enough there, had I suspected any such thing, to have prevented it, but we had not gone many leagues but the news overtook us that Caesar was taken and whipped like a common slave. We met on the river with Colonel Martin, a man of great gallantry, wit and goodness, and whom I have celebrated in a character of my new comedy[152] by his own name, in memory of so brave a man. He was wise and eloquent, and, from the fineness of his parts, bore a great sway over the hearts of all the colony. He was a friend to Caesar, and resented this false dealing with him very much. We carried him back to Parham, thinking to have made an accommodation; when we came, the first news we heard was that the governor was dead of a wound Imoinda had given him, but it was not so well. But it seems he would have the pleasure of beholding the revenge he took on Caesar, and before the cruel ceremony was finished, he dropped down, and then they perceived the wound he had on his shoulder was by a venomed arrow, which, as I said, his Indian mistress healed by sucking the wound.

We were no sooner arrived but we went up to the plantation to see Caesar, whom we found in a very miserable and inexpressable condition, and I have a thousand times admired how he lived, in so much tormenting pain. We said all things to him that trouble, pity and good nature could suggest, protesting our innocence of the fact, and our abhorrence of such cruelties; making a thousand professions and services to him, and begging as many pardons for the offenders, till we said so much that he believed we had no hand in his ill treatment, but told us, he could never pardon Byam. As for Trefry, he confessed he saw his grief and sorrow for his suffering, which he could not hinder, but was like to have been beaten down by the very slaves for speaking in his defence. But for Byam, who was their leader, their head – and should, by his justice and honour, have been an example to them – for him he wished to live, to take a dire revenge of him, and said, *It had been well for him if he had sacrificed me, instead of giving me the contemptible whip.* He refused to talk much, but begging us to give him our hands, he took them and protested never to lift up his to do us any harm. He had a great respect for Colonel Martin and always took his counsel like that of a parent, and assured him, he would obey him in anything but his revenge on Byam. *Therefore,* said he, *for his own safety, let him speedily dispatch me, for if I could dispatch myself, I would not, till that justice were done to my injured person, and the contempt of a soldier. No, I would not kill myself, even after a whipping, but will be content to live with that infamy, and be pointed at by every grinning slave till I have completed my revenge; and then you shall see that Oroonoko scorns to live with the indignity that was put on Caesar.* All we could do could get no more words from him, and we took care to have him put immediately into a healing bath to rid him of his pepper, and ordered a chirurgeon[153] to anoint him with healing balm, which he suffered, and in some time he began to be able to walk and eat. We failed not to visit him every day, and, to that end, had him brought to an apartment at Parham.

The governor was no sooner recovered, and had heard of the menaces of Caesar, but he called his council, who (not to disgrace them, or burlesque the government there) consisted of such notorious villains as Newgate[154] never transported, and possibly originally were such, who understood neither the laws of God or man, and had no sort of principles to make them worthy the name of men. But at the very council table would contradict and fight with one another, and swear so bloodily that it was terrible to hear and see them. (Some of them were afterwards hanged when the Dutch took possession of the place;

others sent off in chains). But calling these special rulers of the nation together, and requiring their counsel in this weighty affair, they all concluded that (damn them) it might be their own cases; and that Caesar ought to be made an example to all the Negroes to fright them from daring to threaten their betters, their lords and masters, and, at this rate, no man was safe from his own slaves, and concluded, *nemine contradicente*,[155] that Caesar should be hanged.

Trefry then thought it time to use his authority, and told Byam, his command did not extend to his lord's plantation, and that Parham was as much exempt from the law as Whitehall;[156] and that they ought no more to touch the servants of the Lord – (who there represented the king's person) than they could those about the king himself; and that Parham was a sanctuary, and though his lord were absent in person, his power was still in being there, which he had entrusted with him, as far as the dominions of his particular plantations reached, and all that belonged to it; the rest of the country, as Byam was lieutenant to his lord, he might exercise his tyranny upon. Trefry had others as powerful, or more, that interested themselves in Caesar's life, and absolutely said, he should be defended. So turning the governor and his wise council out of doors (for they sat at Parham-House), we[157] set a guard upon our landing place, and would admit none but those we called friends to us and Caesar.

The governor having remained wounded at Parham till his recovery was completed, Caesar did not know but he was still there; and indeed, for the most part, his time was spent there for he was one that loved to live at other people's expense, and if he were a day absent, he was ten present there, and used to play, and walk, and hunt, and fish, with Caesar. So that Caesar did not at all doubt, if he once recovered strength, but he should find an opportunity of being revenged on him. Though, after such a revenge, he could not hope to live, for if he escaped the fury of the English mobile,[158] who perhaps would have been glad of the occasion to have killed him, he was resolved not to survive his whipping; yet he had, some tender hours, a repenting softness which he called his fits of coward, wherein he struggled with love for the victory of his heart which took part with his

charming Imoinda there, but, for the most part, his time was
passed in melancholy thought and black designs. He considered,
if he should do this deed, and die either in the attempt or after
it, he left his lovely Imoinda a prey, or at best a slave, to
the enraged multitude; his great heart could not endure that
thought. *Perhaps*, said he, *she may be first ravaged by every
brute, exposed first to their nasty lusts, and then a shameful
death*. No, he could not live a moment under that apprehension,
too insupportable to be borne. These were his thoughts, and his
silent arguments with his heart, as he told us afterwards; so that
now resolving not only to kill Byam, but all those he thought
had enraged him, pleasing his great heart with the fancied
slaughter he should make over the whole face of the plantation.
He first resolved on a deed that (however horrid it first appeared
to us all), when we had heard his reasons, we thought it brave
and just. Being able to walk, and, as he believed, fit for the
execution of his great design, he begged Trefry to trust him into
the air, believing a walk would do him good; which was granted
him, and taking Imoinda with him, as he used to do in his more
happy and calmer days, he led her up into a wood, where, after
(with a thousand sighs and long gazing silently on her face,
while tears gushed, in spite of him, from his eyes), he told her
his design first of killing her, and then his enemies, and next
himself, and the impossibility of escaping, and therefore he told
her the necessity of dying. He found the heroic wife faster
pleading for death than he was to propose it when she found his
fixed resolution, and, on her knees, besought him not to leave
her a prey to his enemies. He (grieved to death) yet pleased at
her noble resolution, took her up, and embracing her with all
the passion and languishment of a dying lover, drew his knife
to kill this treasure of his soul, this pleasure of his eyes. While
tears trickled down his cheeks, hers were smiling with joy she
should die by so noble a hand and be sent in her own country
(for that is their notion of the next world) by him she so tenderly
loved and so truly adored in this; for wives have a respect for
their husbands equal to what any other people pay a deity, and
when a man finds any occasion to quit his wife, if he love her,
she dies by his hand, if not, he sells her, or suffers some other to

kill her. It being thus, you may believe the deed was soon resolved on, and it is not to be doubted but the parting, the eternal leave-taking of two such lovers, so greatly born, so sensible,[159] so beautiful, so young and so fond, must be very moving, as the relation of it was to be afterwards.

All that love could say in such cases being ended, and all the intermitting irresolutions being adjusted, the lovely, young and adored victim lays herself down before the sacrificer, while he, with a hand resolved and a heart breaking within, gave the fatal stroke,[160] first cutting her throat, and then severing her yet smiling face from that delicate body, pregnant as it was with the fruits of tenderest love. As soon as he had done, he laid the body decently on leaves and flowers, of which he made a bed, and concealed it under the same coverlid of Nature, only her face he left yet bare to look on. But when he found she was dead and past all retrieve, never more to bless him with her eyes and soft language, his grief swelled up to rage; he tore, he raved, he roared like some monster of the wood, calling on the loved name of Imoinda. A thousand times he turned the fatal knife that did the deed toward his own heart, with a resolution to go immediately after her, but dire revenge, which was now a thousand times more fierce in his soul than before, prevents him, and he would cry out, *No, since I have sacrificed Imoinda to my revenge, shall I lose that glory which I have purchased so dear, as the price of the fairest, dearest, softest creature that ever Nature made? No, no!* Then, at her name, grief would get the ascendant of rage, and he would lie down by her side, and water her face with showers of tears, which never were wont to fall from those eyes. And however bent he was on his intended slaughter, he had not power to stir from the sight of this dear object, now more beloved and more adored than ever.

He remained in this deploring condition for two days, and never rose from the ground where he had made his sad sacrifice. At last, rousing from her side, and accusing himself of living too long now Imoinda was dead, and that the deaths of those barbarous enemies were deferred too long, he resolved now to finish the great work; but offering to rise, he found his strength so decayed that he reeled to and fro like boughs assailed by contrary winds, so that he was forced to lie down again and try to summon all his courage to his aid. He found his brains turned round, and his eyes were dizzy, and objects appeared not the same to him [as] they were wont to do; his breath was short, and all his limbs surprised with a faintness he had never felt before. He had not eaten in two days, which was one occasion of his feebleness, but excess of grief was the greatest; yet still he hoped he should recover vigour to act his design, and lay expecting it yet six days longer, still mourning over the dead idol of his heart, and striving every day to rise but could not.

In all this time you may believe we were in no little affliction for Caesar and his wife. Some were of opinion he was escaped never to return; others thought some accident had happened to him. But however, we failed not to send out a hundred people several ways to search for him. A party of about forty went that way he took, among whom was Tuscan, who was perfectly reconciled to Byam. They had not gone very far into the wood, but they smelt an unusual smell, as of a dead body, for stinks must be very noisome that can be distinguished among such a quantity of natural sweets as every inch of that land produces. So that they concluded they should find him dead, or somebody that was so. They passed on towards it, as loathsome as it was, and made such rustling among the leaves that lie thick on the ground by continual falling that Caesar heard he was approached; and though he had, during the space of these eight days, endeavoured to rise, but found he wanted strength, yet looking up and seeing his pursuers, he rose and reeled to a neighbouring tree, against which he fixed his back. And being within a dozen yards of those that advanced and saw him, he called out to them, and bid them approach no nearer if they would be safe, so that they stood still, and hardly believing their eyes that would persuade them that it was Caesar that spoke to them, so much was he altered. They asked him, what he had done with his wife? for they smelt a stink that almost struck them dead. He, pointing to the dead body, sighing, cried, *Behold her there*. They put off the flowers that covered her with their sticks, and found she was killed, and cried out, *O monster! that hast murdered thy wife*. Then asking him, why he did so cruel a deed, he replied, he had no leisure to answer impertinent questions. *You may go back*, continued he, *and tell the faithless governor, he may thank fortune that I am breathing my last, and that my arm is too feeble to obey my heart in what it had designed him.* But his tongue faltering and trembling, he could scarce end what he was saying. The English taking advantage of his weakness, cried, *Let us take him alive by all means.* He heard them; and, as if he had revived from a fainting or a dream, he cried out, *No, gentlemen, you are deceived, you will find no more Caesars to be whipped, no more find a faith in me. Feeble as you think me, I have strength yet left to secure me from a second indignity.* They swore all anew, and he only shook his head, and beheld them with scorn. Then they cried out, *Who will venture on this single man? Will nobody?* They stood all silent while Caesar replied, *Fatal will be the attempt to the first adventurer, let him assure himself*, and, at that word, held up his knife in a menacing posture. *Look ye, ye faithless crew*, said he, *it is not life I seek, nor am I afraid of dying*, and, at that word, cut a piece of flesh from his own throat, and threw it at them, *yet still I would live if I could till I had perfected my revenge. But oh! it cannot be. I feel life gliding from my eyes and heart, and, if I make not haste, I shall fall a victim to the shameful whip.* At that, he ripped up his own belly, and took his bowels and pulled them out with what strength he could, while some, on their knees imploring, besought him to hold his hand. But when they saw him tottering, they cried out, *Will none venture on him?* A bold English cried, *Yes, if he were the Devil* (taking courage when he saw him almost dead), and, swearing a horrid oath for his farewell to the world, he rushed on. Caesar with his armed hand met him so fairly, as stuck him to the heart, and he fell dead at his feet.[161] Tuscan seeing that, cried out, *I love thee, O Caesar! and therefore will not let thee die, if possible.* And, running to him, took him in his arms, but, at the same time, warding a blow that Caesar made at his bosom, he received it quite through his arm, and Caesar having not the strength to pluck the knife forth, though he attempted it, Tuscan neither pulled it out himself nor suffered it to be pulled out, but

came down with it sticking in his arm, and the reason he gave
for it was, because the air should not get into the wound. They
put their hands across, and carried Caesar between six of them,
fainted as he was and they thought dead or just dying; and they
brought him to Parham, and laid him on a couch, and had the
chirurgeon immediately to him, who dressed his wounds and
sewed up his belly, and used means to bring him to life, which
they effected. We ran all to see him; and, if before we thought
him so beautiful a sight, he was now so altered that his face was
like a death's head blacked over, nothing but teeth and eye-holes.
For some days we suffered nobody to speak to him, but caused
cordials to be poured down his throat, which sustained his life,
and in six or seven days he recovered his senses. For you must
know, that wounds are almost to a miracle cured in the Indies,
unless wounds in the legs which rarely ever cure.

When he was well enough to speak, we talked to him, and
asked him some questions about his wife, and the reasons why
he killed her. And he then told us what I have related of that
resolution and of his parting, and he besought us, we would let
him die, and was extremely afflicted to think it was possible he
might live. He assured us, if we did not dispatch him, he would
prove very fatal to a great many. We said all we could to make
him live, and gave him new assurances, but he begged we would
not think so poorly of him, or of his love to Imoinda, to imagine
we could flatter him to life again; but the chirurgeon assured him,
he could not live, and therefore he need not fear. We were all (but
Caesar) afflicted at this news, and the sight was ghashly.[162] His
discourse was sad; and the earthy smell about him was so strong
that I was persuaded to leave the place for some time (being myself
but sickly, and very apt to fall into fits of dangerous illness upon
any extraordinary melancholy).[163] The servants and Trefry and
the chirurgeons promised all to take what possible care they could
of the life of Caesar, and I, taking boat, went with other company
to Colonel Martin's, about three days' journey down the river;
but I was no sooner gone than the governor taking Trefry about
some pretended earnest business a day's journey up the river,
having communicated his design to one Banister,[164] a wild

Irishman and one of the council, a fellow of absolute barbarity, and fit to execute any villainy, but was rich. He came up to Parham, and forcibly took Caesar, and had him carried to the same post where he was whipped, and causing him to be tied to it,[165] and a great fire made before him, he told him, he should die like a dog as he was. Caesar replied, this was the first piece of bravery that ever Banister did, and he never spoke sense till he pronounced that word, and, if he would keep it, he would declare, in the other world, that he was the only man, of all the whites, that ever he heard speak truth. And turning to the men that had bound him, he said, *My friends, am I to die, or to be whipped?* And they cried, *Whipped! no, you shall not escape so well.* And then he replied, smiling, *A blessing on thee*, and assured them they need not tie him, for he would stand fixed like a rock, and endure death so as should encourage them to die. *But if you whip me*, said he, *be sure you tie me fast.*

He had learned to take tobacco, and when he was assured he should die, he desired they would give him a pipe[166] in his mouth, ready lighted which they did, and the executioner came and first cut off his members and threw them into the fire. After that, with an ill-favoured knife, they cut his ears and his nose, and burned them; he still smoked on, as if nothing had touched him. Then they hacked off one of his arms, and still he bore up, and held his pipe. But at the cutting off the other arm, his head sunk, and his pipe dropped, and he gave up the ghost[167] without a groan or a reproach.[168] My mother and sister were by him all the while but not suffered to save him, so rude and wild were the rabble, and so inhuman were the justices who stood by to see the execution, who after paid dearly enough for their insolence. They cut Caesar in quarters, and sent them to several of the chief plantations. One quarter was sent to Colonel Martin, who refused it, and swore he had rather see the quarters of Banister and the governor himself than those of Caesar, on his plantations; and that he could govern his Negroes without terrifying and grieving them with frightful spectacles of a mangled king.

Thus died this great man, worthy of a better fate and a more sublime wit than mine to write his praise. Yet, I hope, the reputation of my pen is considerable enough to make his glorious name to survive to all ages, with that of the brave, the beautiful and the constant Imoinda.

FINIS.

Notes

The following abbreviations are used in the Notes:

Biet   Antoine Biet, *Voyage de la France équixonale en l'isle de Cayenne* (1654)
du Tertre   Jean-Baptiste du Tertre, *Histoire Générale Des Antilles habitées par les François*, 4 vols. (1667)
Ogilby   John Ogilby, *America: Being the Latest, and Most Accurate Description of the New World* (1671)
Tryon   Thomas Tryon, *Friendly Advice to the Gentlemen-Planters of the East and West Indies* (1684)
Warren   George Warren, *Impartial Description of Surinam upon The Continent of Guiana in America* (1667)
Works   *The Works of Aphra Behn*, ed. Janet Todd, 7 vols. (London: William Pickering, 1992–6)

The Epistle Dedicatory To the Right Honourable the Lord Maitland

1. *Maitland*: Richard Lord Maitland (1653–95) was one of the unpopular Scottish ministers on whom King James II relied in the last months of his reign. Although the nephew of the Protestant Duke of Lauderdale, who had ruled Scotland autocratically in the 1670s, Maitland, like the poet laureate John Dryden, was a recent Catholic convert. After James II's fall he fled to the Continent and became part of the exiled court; later he objected to James's extreme Catholic views and was banished. Behn praises Maitland for his scholarly and literary activities; he would translate Virgil's *Aeneid* and Dryden claimed he consulted this translation when making his own version.
2. *nice*: Fastidious, sensitive.
3. *agreements*: Attractions.
4. *gust*: Taste.

5. *elevated parts*: Exalted qualities.

6. *gownmen*: Clergymen.

7. *instruct the ignorant*: The inclusion in one version of *Oroonoko* of the lines beginning 'Where is it amongst all our nobility' and concluding with 'instruct the ignorant!' has fuelled claims that Behn was herself a Catholic although they clearly form part of her flattery of Lord Maitland. If the copy including the lines was an early one, it is possible that, after publication in June or July 1688 (that is, just after the controversial birth of the Prince of Wales and the rumours that he was not the queen's son but a baby brought in within a warming-pan to ensure the Catholic succession), Behn or possibly her publisher William Canning thought better of so public an endorsement of Catholicism and excised the passage.

8. *St Augustine*: St Augustine of Hippo (AD 354–430), a North African theologian and Church father. He studied in Carthage, Rome and Milan, converting to Manichaeism and scepticism for a short time. Augustine was thirty-two when he re-converted to Christianity and returned to North Africa, where he founded a monastic community. He was an active participant in the Pelagian controversy, insisting that Original Sin did exist and that man needed divine grace to attain eternal life. Behn may have been rather wryly considering this in her allusion to Augustine, as she constantly refers to Paradise and the Fall of Adam in *Oroonoko*.

9. *incommode*: Inconvenient (French).

10. *most illustrious family*: In 1678 Maitland had married Anne Campbell, the daughter of the ultra-Protestant Earl of Argyll, recently executed for his rebellious activities against Charles II and James II. Behn makes a parallel between Maitland and his wife and her hero and heroine in *Oroonoko*.

THE HISTORY OF THE ROYAL SLAVE

1. *without ... invention*: In the French romance *Cassandra*, published between 1644 and 1650 and widely read by Behn and her contemporaries, the playwright and novelist La Calprenède claimed to be telling historical truth and assured his readers that he did not contradict history in 'those accidents that are feign'd'. Within it the story of Oroondates, a Scythian prince resembling Oroonoko, was told by a squire who claimed he had heard or seen all that was related.

2. *eye-witness ... here set down*: Although her presence there has

sometimes been doubted, Aphra Behn seems to have arrived in Surinam in mid or late 1663 and left in 1664. Much of the description of the country is probably from memory, perhaps overlaid by accounts such as that in Warren.

3. *Surinam*: (Present-day Suriname) An English colony on the northern coast of South America, first settled in the 1640s and more securely established in the 1650s by Anthony Rous and Francis, Lord Willoughby of Parham (1613?–66), who wrote a prospectus for the new settlement, *Certain overtures made by the Lord Willoughby of Parham unto all such as shall incline to plant in the Colony of Surinam* (*c.* 1662–5). Willoughby's colony was situated between the rivers Saramacca and Marowyne, and its capital, Tararica, was on the banks of the Surinam River.

4. *cousheries*: Animals mentioned in several travel accounts. According to Warren (p. 14) the cusharee was black and lived in trees, was shaped like a lion and was smaller than a marmoset. Ogilby (p. 618) says it was about the 'bigness' of a little dog with the shape of a lion. Despite its existence in Biet's Galibi dictionary, the word might derive from Portuguese since 'cujaree' is Portuguese/Brazilian for the rice rat.

5. *a thousand other birds ... colours*: Ogilby (p. 618), echoing much of Warren's detail, wrote, '*Guiana* produces ... strange fowls, amongst which the chiefest are a sort whose feathers glitter like Scarlet, and walk along in Rank and Fyle like Soldiers.'

6. *his Majesty's Antiquaries*: This is probably a reference to the Royal Society's museum. The Royal Society acquired 'rarities' of various kinds in its earliest years, the first dated gift in the extant catalogue being made on 18 May 1661, though the 'Repository' for the possessions was founded in 1666. Among the items catalogued in 1679 was 'An Indian Peruque, made not of hair but feather, a mantle also of feathers.'

7. *flies*: Butterflies. Warren (p. 6) notes butterflies with 'fair painted black and Saffron-Coloured Wings'. He wrote that, 'having lived a while, [this butterfly] at length lights upon the ground, takes Root, and is transformed into a Plant': he had this 'Information of the Honourable *William Byam*, Lord General of *Guiana*, and Governour of *Surinam*, who, I am sure is too much a Gentleman to be the Author of a Lie'.

8. *King's Theatre*: Run by Thomas Killigrew (with Dryden as one of its playwrights); it relied much on spectacular props and scenery.

9. *the Indian Queen*: An heroic play by Dryden and Sir Robert Howard, portraying fictitious events in the youth of Montezuma.

Its success was partly due to its exotic décor and costumes, which included 'habits of white and red Feathers' for sacrificial priests. The diarist Pepys records that the streets near the theatre were 'full of coaches at the new play, *The Indian Queen*; which for show, they say, exceeds *Henry the 8th*' (27 January 1664: *The Diary of Samuel Pepys*, ed. Robert Latham and William Matthews (London: G. Bell and Hyman, 1971), 5.28–9). The first performance (before 25 January 1664) predates Behn's probable return from Surinam, but she may have provided feathers to adorn the play's titular villainess in a revival; one is recorded in 1668. Costumes and scenery from *The Indian Queen* were recycled in its sequel, Dryden's *The Indian Emperor* (1665), while an operatic version of *The Indian Queen*, with music by Henry and Daniel Purcell, was premièred in 1695, a decade in which there was a fashion for 'Indian' subjects helped by the success of Southerne's *Oroonoko*. In *The Widdow Ranter* (1690) Behn herself created an Indian Queen, the virtuous and vulnerable Semernia. An illustration of the actress Anne Bracegirdle in this role shows her wearing a feather head-dress. If the gift of the feathers is a true detail, presumably Behn had hoped that she might benefit from it by finding a home in the King's Theatre for her play *The Young King* (1683), which she claimed was 'the first Essay of my Infant-Poetry', written when she feared the 'reproach of being an *American*' (*Works* 7.83).

10. *ell*: The English ell measured 45 inches.

11. *unadorned*: Behn describes the Native Americans as both 'naked' and covered in aprons, beads and paint. The natural lack of shame is a usual feature of her depiction of a Golden Age world. It can be found in many pastoral writers and is a convention of the tradition expressed by Torquato Tasso in his poem 'O bella eta de l'oro' (from *Aminta*, 1573) and in Behn's own adaptation, 'The Golden Age' (1684; *Works* 1.30–35), where it coexists with open sexual expression.

12. *before the Fall*: Adam and Eve as described in Genesis before they were expelled from the Garden of Eden. The myth had been given extra currency by Milton's recently published *Paradise Lost*.

13. *knows no fraud*: Ernest Bernbaum in 'Mrs Aphra Behn's Biography a Fiction', *PMLA*, 28 (1913), 432–53, claims that the Indians had in fact five distinct words for falsehood. Warren (p. 23) insisted on the Indians' capacity for treachery. In contrast to Behn's presentation of a lying governor, Biet (p. 263) praised deputy governor Byam as a good man who kept his word.

14. *conduct*: Ability to command.
15. *we live . . . good understanding*: Lord Willoughby's letter to his wife mentions 'Indian kings . . . who are all willing to receive our nation, and that we shall settle amongst them', *Memorials of the Great Civil War in England from 1646 to 1652* (1842), pp. 316–17.
16. *savannahs*: Open grasslands usually found in the tropics and subtropics. Willoughby's letter to his wife mentions Surinam's 'brave savanas, where you may, in coach or on horseback, ride thirty or forty miles'. Behn also uses the term in *The Widdow Ranter* (*Works* 7.305).
17. *ours*: Behn is careful with pronouns when referring to the Europeans. Often she uses 'we' and accepts herself as part of this group, as when she refers to their vulnerable position in Surinam, but, at other times, when the Europeans are acting with deceit not justified by their vulnerability, she distinguishes herself from them and uses the pronoun 'they'.
18. *by lot*: R. Ligon claimed dealers chose individually, paying £30 for the 'best man Negre', *True and Exact History of the Island of Barbados* (1657), p. 46.
19. *Coramantien*: (Koromantyn) A fort and trading post on the west coast of Africa, a few miles east of modern Cape Coast in Ghana. With agreement from the local Fanti chiefs it was established by the English just before 1630 (then taken by the Dutch and retaken by the English); the name was employed loosely for most of the coast of modern Ghana and for the slaves from there, who were much prized. These came mainly from the Fanti, Ashanti and interior tribes. In the 1660s the actual post was used by the English and Dutch slave-traders.
20. *his successor one grandchild*: Neither Behn nor her adapters can imagine anything like the African system of matrilineal descent. English male primogeniture simply becomes the norm.
21. *field of Mars*: The battlefield; Mars was the god of war.
22. *Oroonoko*: The name may be derived from the South American river the Orinoco, which meets the sea in Venezuela. The name of the river is spelt 'Oronoque' in the contemporary *London Gazette* and frequently 'Oroonoko' in the eighteenth century. In Yoruba (from Nigeria) one of the gods is called Oro and there are names such as Okonkwo which resemble Oroonoko, but Behn's slave is more likely to be from Ashanti. The name also recalls the romance names for exotic princely characters such as Oroondates, see note 1.

23. *Moor*: Latin *Mauros* was applied to people belonging to the mixed Berber and Arab race inhabiting Mauritania (NW Africa, now parts of Morocco and Algeria). By the time of Shakespeare's *Titus Andronicus* (?1590) the term 'Moor' was used for both sub-Saharan Africans, or 'Blackamoors', and North Africans; sometimes it solely denoted the former while some North Africans were referred to as 'Turks' or 'white Moors'.

24. *that of the Spaniards*: In fact it was the Portuguese who provided a common trading language on the West African coast.

25. *Civil Wars . . . death of our great monarch*: The wars of the 1640s between Royalists and Parliamentarians, culminating in the execution of Charles I in 1649. With this allusion Behn in 1688 was signalling her support for James II, Charles I's son.

26. *statuary*: Sculptor of statues.

27. *awful*: Commanding, impressive.

28. *Bating*: Except for.

29. *nothing in nature . . . handsome*: Although realizing that each race had its peculiar standard of beauty, seventeenth-century European writers rarely found it completely possible to appreciate African features – cf. the description of Moorea in Behn's 'The Unfortunate Bride' (1700; *Works* 3.319–34).

30. *politic*: Sagacious or shrewd.

31. *Venus . . . Mars*: The goddess of love and god of war, who, in mythology, were lovers.

32. *awfulness*: Awe.

33. *admired*: Wondered.

34. *conversation*: Company.

35. *the gods*: The religions of West Africa seem to have lacked a systematic body of doctrines. They tended to assume a supreme being, but more important were lesser powers associated with particular local natural phenomena. Dead ancestors were believed to have much influence on the lives of the living and they could act as intermediaries between the people and the gods. Behn may have learnt of African belief systems in Surinam or she may have been drawing on classical mythology.

36. *burnt*: Burned with passion.

37. *injuring him*: Taking her virginity and so robbing him of a husband's rights.

38. *objected to him*: Protested or made this objection to him.

39. *otan*: Since this section seems inspired by oriental tales and is more reminiscent of European ideas of the East than of Africa,

perhaps the word derives from *oda*, the Turkish term for a room in a seraglio, or the Persian *otagh*, a tent or pavilion. In the Akan languages of the Gold Coast, *odammaa* and *odan* signify a small hut or room. See D. M. Warren, *Bibliography and Vocabulary of the Akan Languages of Ghana* (Bloomington: Indiana University Press, 1976), and J. G. Christaller, *Dictionary of the Asante and Fanti Languages* (1881).

40. *son*: In fact grandson.

41. *cast mistresses*: Cast off, discarded mistresses.

42. *governants*: Governesses.

43. *despites*: Insults.

44. *antic*: Grotesque, wild.

45. *a rest of*: A remainder.

46. *ravished . . . for so many months*: This outwitting of age by youth is a stock comic trope; a similar situation is described in Dryden's comedy *The Assignation; Or, Love in a Nunnery* (1673), itself a retelling of one of Marie-Catherine Hortense Desjardins's *The Annals of Love* (1671). In Behn's fiction the action occurs in two stories, *Love-Letters between a Nobleman and his Sister* (1684–7; *Works* 2) and *The Lucky Mistake* (1689; *Works* 3), as well as in many of her plays such as *Sir Patient Fancy* (1678; *Works* 6). In this example Oroonoko for a moment assumes the glamour of the comic rake.

47. *disobliged*: Offended.

48. *repent him*: Repent, regret.

49. *maugre*: In spite of.

50. *constitute*: Appoint.

51. *he leapt from his couch*: This is the first of many parallels between Oroonoko and classical heroes, here Achilles in the *Iliad*, who, after withdrawing from the battle against the Trojans when his female prize is denied him, returns when his friend Patrocles is killed. He then triumphs in battle.

52. *wrecking*: Racking.

53. *put on him*: Reads 'put him on' in all early editions.

54. *effects*: The original reads 'efforts'.

55. *mediums*: Moderation, compromise.

56. *This person*: The commander of the ship.

57. *betrayed to slavery*: The kidnapping of African slave-traders or their sons was a recorded and condemned practice, often undertaken to obtain ransom. See the missionary to the Antilles, du Tertre (2.494), where he describes unjust merchants who take

those 'qui étoient venus à leur vaisseau pour y faire bone chere:
& l'on m'a dit, qu'un certain Capitaine en ayat attiré plusieurs
dans son vaisseau à force de boisson & de presens, pendant que
ces pauvres gens ne songeoient qu'à se bien divertir; le Pilote
ayant levé l'anchre, si-tost que le Navire fut sous voile, on les
saisit, & chargea de chaisnes, & qu'ils furent amenés aux Isles,
où ils furent vendus en qualité d'esclaves' (who came on board in
good faith, and I've heard that one captain persuaded through
drinking and gifts several on to his ship; while these poor people
thought only of pleasure, the pilot raised the anchor and as soon
as the ship was under sail they were seized, put in irons and taken
to the islands where they were sold as slaves). Nothing on the
scale Behn describes here is noted in English documents of the
early 1660s.

58.   *parole*: Word or pledge.

59.   *generous not*: The 1688 edition has a comma between these two
words which renders the qualifying clause critical of Oroonoko
but then makes the whole sentence difficult to interpret.

60.   *pickaninnies*: Young West Indian children of African descent.
The word is probably derived from the Portuguese diminutive
pequenino meaning 'very small'.

61.   *true knowledge ... your gods*: Tryon (pp. 161–87) stressed the
unchristian behaviour of many slave-traders. Behn knew Tryon
and wrote a commendatory poem for his book *The Way to
Health, Long Life, and Happiness* (*Works* 1.179–80).

62.   *Lord* — : Trefry seems to have been Lord Willoughby's agent or
overseer in his Surinam plantation of Parham as well as managing
St John's Hill. Although in a letter of 1662 Trefry calls Byam
'our noble Governor' (*Historical Manuscripts Commission, 10th
Report*, 6, Bouverie MSS), in *Oroonoko* Behn pits Trefry against
deputy governor Byam, who misuses his authority in Willoughby's absence.

63.   *vest*: Robe.

64.   *backearay*: Possibly a variant of *buckra* or *bakra* ('master'), the
word used in Surinam by the Africans for the Europeans; see J. A.
Ramsaram, 'Oroonoko: A Study of the Factual Elements', *Notes
and Queries*, 205 (1969), 142–5. Cf. 'Bachararo's, so the Negro's
in their Language call the Whites', Tryon, p. 151.

65.   *the river*: Surinam River was lined with plantations; its navigation
was difficult and required different sorts of boats at different
places.

66.   *osenbrigs ... brown Holland*: Coarse cotton or linen, also called

Osnaburg, or the variant Osenbrig, from the north German town Osnabrück, noted for its manufacture of linen.

67. *some name of their own*: It was common for slave-owners to give slaves Roman names in part to parallel contemporary society with that of the slave-owning Romans. The use of the name 'Caesar' here, after the Roman conqueror Julius Caesar, makes more overt the parallel between the noble and ill-fated slave and James II, frequently referred to by Behn in her poems as 'Caesar'. Julius Caesar was betrayed by his friends and stabbed to death.

68. *wanted*: Lacked.

69. *female pen . . . his fame*: Behn frequently laments the situation of the female writer by alluding to the inadequate philosophical and classical education of women. Cf. 'To the Unknown Daphnis and his Excellent Translation of Lucretius' (*Works* 1.25) where she writes:

> Till now I curst my Sex and *Education*,
> And more the Scanted Customs of the Nation,
> Permitting not the Female Sex to tread
> The Mighty Paths of Learned *Heroes* Dead.

70. *The Dutch . . . time*: The Dutch captured Surinam in February 1667; it was retaken by the English in October but was ceded to the Dutch at the Treaty of Breda. Trefry remained in Surinam and was one of those for whom Bannister (see note 164) was trying to get a ship after the Dutch takeover. He seems to have died around 1674.

71. *Parham House*: Part of Lord Willoughby's estate of Parham Hill.

72. *grandee*: Spanish nobleman, here simply an important man.

73. *Clemene*: The name is possibly derived from the Latin *clementia*, meaning 'clemency' or 'gentleness'. Imoinda is only partly assimilated into a European culture and the pastoral name Clemene is seldom used.

74. *God of Day*: The sun god, Apollo, pursued and tried to rape the nymph Daphne.

75. *notions of honour . . . in her*: Black African women were not usually treated with such reverence as Imoinda inspired, but see du Tertre (2.495–6), who described one thus: 'Elle avoit un port de Reyne, & un esprit si élevé au dessus de la misere de sa condition, qu'on voyoit bien qu'elle n'avoit rien perdu de sa dignité, dans sa disgrace. Tous les autres Négres de sa terre,

hommes & femmes, luy rendoient des respects comme à une
Princesse; quand ils la voyoient à l'Eglise ou en chemin, ils s'arres-
toient tout court devant elle, ils mettoient les deux mains à terre,
& s'en frappoient les cuisses, & les tenoient en un moment élevées
au dessus se leurs restes, qui est la maniere dont ils rendent
homage à leurs Souverains' (She had the demeanour of a queen,
and a spirit so elevated above the misery of her condition, that it
was clear that she had lost nothing of her dignity in her disgrace.
All the other negroes of her country, men and women, paid her
their respects as they would a princess; when they saw her at
church or out walking, they stopped in front of her, put both
their hands on the earth, slapped their thighs and then raised their
hands above their heads, which is the manner with which they
pay tribute to their sovereigns).

76. *shock-dog*: A poodle or fashionable dog with long shaggy hair.
    Later editions changed 'Clemene' to 'Trefry' to make the meaning
    clearer.

77. *allay*: Abatement, diminution.

78. *novel*: New turn in events. The reunion scene is pure romance,
    paralleled by reunions in countless tales including those of La
    Calprenède.

79. *raced*: Incised.

80. *japanned . . . flowers*: Unlike usual geometric African tribal marks
    from the Gold Coast, Imoinda's presumed home, hers are in the
    aesthetic forms appreciated by Europeans, so that her body seems
    like Japanese lacquerwork. It was some years since Behn had been
    in Surinam and her notion of slavery probably had more to do
    with the East where slaves, often Christians, could be regarded
    as treasured objects rather than work-horses.

81. *Picts*: The Picts (possibly from the Latin for 'painted people')
    were ancient people from North Britain who painted or tattooed
    themselves. They are described in such contemporary chronicles
    as *Britannia Speculum* (1683). The engravings of Picts in Thomas
    Hariot's *A Brief and True Report of the New Found Land of
    Virginia* (1588) are accompanied by the comment that the mark-
    ings of the Picts were similar to those of the Native Americans in
    Virginia.

82. *all the breed . . . parents belong*: This was the defining difference
    between African slaves and European slaves or indentured ser-
    vants held on European plantations, that since the former were
    considered aliens or non-citizens as well as infidels their children
    would be slaves also.

83. *jealousies*: Suspicions.
84. *mutiny*: This was a constant fear in the Caribbean and South American colonies.
85. *lives of the Romans*: Plutarch's *Lives*, in particular his account of Julius Caesar, was extremely popular in the seventeenth century and many translations appeared in Behn's lifetime, some prefaced with exhortations to heroism since Plutarch served in many ways as a handbook of approved male character. Plutarch did not include the heroic courtly love that Oroonoko displays, but the theme was later grafted on to the heroic tradition he established. In the context of a mismanaged colony of people of lowly birth, the work with which the narrator entertained Oroonoko was politically subversive.
86. *pretty works*: Fine sewing and embroidery.
87. *stories of nuns*: Possibly Behn may be alluding to one of her own novels, of which many revolve around nuns and their amorous adventures. *The Fair Jilt* (1688; *Works* 3), published in the same year as *Oroonoko*, has a nun, Miranda, as the leading female character, a villainous woman who ends triumphant; the following year Behn's *History of the Nun* (1689; *Works* 3), which ends with a nun's execution for bigamy and murder, was published. So perhaps Imoinda's tales were as subversive as Oroonoko's.
88. *pitching the bar*: Throwing a heavy bar was a form of athletic exercise at this time especially for soldiers. See Thomas D'Urfey, *Wit and Mirth: or, Pills to purge Melancholy* (6 vols.; 1719–20), 3.253, 4: 'I . . . can . . . pitch-bar, and run and wrestle too.'
89. *tigers*: Used not only for modern African tigers but also for South American jaguars and pumas. Ogilby (p. 618) writes: 'The Tygers here are either black, spotted, or red; the spotted and red devour abundance of Cattel, but will seldom set upon a Man, especially in the day-time.'
90. *river of Amazons*: The Amazons were a mythical race of female warriors. Alexander the Great's encounter with Thallestris, the Queen of the Amazons, was frequently recorded though it is treated with scepticism by historians such as Plutarch. Other historians portray Alexander conquering the area around the River Jaxartes, supposedly the home of the Amazons, and the accounts describe gleaming poisonous snakes. By the seventeenth century, Alexander had been the subject of innumerable romances. In one of the earliest, the *Alexander Romance* (c. AD 300) by pseudo-Callisthenes, the hero meets river snakes on his lengthy quest-adventure. See also La Calprenède's *Cassandra*.

Warren (pp. 20–21) and Ogilby (p. 618) note the huge water snakes of Surinam.

91. *my father died at sea*: There is no corroboration of this account by Behn of her father's position but, if he is indeed the Bartholomew Johnson described by Jane Jones in 'New Light on the Background and Early Life of Aphra Behn' (*Notes and Queries*, 235 (1990), 288–93), he may have left Kent with his family and died at sea, as the real governor Willoughby was about to do.

92. *lieutenant-general*: Willoughby had powers under Charles II to appoint deputies in civil and military capacities. William Byam was both deputy governor and in late 1663 lieutenant-general.

93. *continent*: Any area not an island.

94. *his late Majesty*: Charles II had died in 1685.

95. *parted . . . with it to the Dutch*: See notes 70, 129 and 130.

96. *Spring . . . Autumn*: Warren (p. 5) notes that 'There is a constant Spring and Fall . . . Some [trees] have always Blossoms, and the several degrees of fruit at once', and Ogilby (p. 617), 'No Plant is ever seen here without either Leaf, Blossom, or Fruit, except the *European* Apple-Tree, which never changes its nature, but blossoms and bears Fruit at the same time of the year as in *Europe*'. The identification Behn made of Surinam with Arcadia becomes even clearer in what she omitted. Most settlers were forcefully struck by the dank, torrid heat and by mosquitoes, which could only be avoided by burning tobacco leaves.

97. *armadillo . . . six weeks old*: See *Life and Food in the Caribbean* (London: Weidenfeld and Nicolson, 1991), where Cristine Mackie notes that the native meat they used would have been tatoo (armadillo), agouti (like a rabbit with long legs), bush hogs and labba (large guinea pigs).

98. *St John's Hill*: One of three plantations owned by the absentee landlord Sir Robert Harley, Willoughby's friend and now chancellor of Barbados. Harley had bought the plantation from Byam, and the Cornishman John Trefry appears to have been managing it among his other duties. The estate was close to Parham Hill, Willoughby's estate on the banks of the Surinam River. A letter dated 27 January 1664 from one of Harley's employees, William Yearworth (BL Add.MS 70010), indicates the presence of ladies at the time Behn claims to have been there. Possibly Harley had sold the estate to Willoughby in 1663 or 1664.

99. *blowing*: Flowering.

100. *ravishing . . . sands*: The 1688 edition reads 'raving'; it was

changed to 'ravishing' in the third edition. In some later editions
'sands' became 'fancy', but this seems an unnecessary change.

101. *Mall*: The first two editions read 'Marl'; the third emends this to
'mall', presumably a reference to the Mall in London, a fashionable walk along one side of St James's Park.

102. *flowery and fruity branches meet*: The 1688 edition reads 'fruity
bear branches meet'; the third edition emends this to 'fruit-bearing
branches met'.

103. *her nest ... he*: There seems some confusion over the animal's
sex. Later editions emend the pronouns to make the tiger female
throughout. The next tiger mentioned is similarly ambiguous.

104. *the great Oliverian*: Henry Martin or Marten (1602–80) was not
a follower of Oliver Cromwell (an Oliverian), but an ardent
republican who opposed Cromwell's protectorate. He was also
one of the judges who signed the death warrant of Charles I and
was imprisoned as a regicide at the Restoration. The older Behn
cannot have approved his politics but she may have liked his
engaging book of letters entitled *Coll. Henry Marten's Familiar
Letters to his Lady of Delight* (1662), written while he was in the
Tower. When in her play *The Roundheads* (1681; *Works* 6)
Behn mocked the parliamentarians from the Interregnum, she
mentioned but did not portray Henry Marten, although he was
elsewhere the butt of satirists for his politics and womanizing.
George Marten, a younger brother, had probably been a settler
and assembly member in Barbados; in the late 1650s he trans-
ferred to Surinam, on whose map there are plantations bearing
the name 'Marten'. He died there in 1666.

105. *This heart ... brought up to us*: This was the kind of valiant act
frequent in the pages of La Calprenède's romances. In Warren
(pp. 12–13), the outcome of such an encounter is less heroic: a
man wanting very much to 'meet with a *Tyger*' does so and is
killed by it.

106. *numb eel*: Electric eel. See Warren (p. 2), 'the *Torpedo* or *Num-
Eele*, which, being alive, and touching any other Living Creature,
strikes ... a deadness into all the parts', and Ogilby (p. 618),
'Here are also great Fishes call'd *Manati* and *Num-Eel*, by which
if any part of a Man be touch'd, it immediately becomes stiff'.
See also *The Diary of John Evelyn* (18 March 1680) where he
records receiving 'a letter from Surenam of a certaine small Eele
that being taken with hook and line ... did so benumb, and
stupifie the limbs of the Fisher'.

107. *philosophy*: Idea or explanation.

108. *remained . . . a league*: Travelled about three miles.

109. *cut in pieces . . . nailed him to trees*: Warren (p. 26) described the cruelty of the Native Americans to those they captured, but he noted too their reluctance to attack English settlers after the initial encounters.

110. *commode*: Suitable. It is hard to see such elaborate costumes as wholly appropriate for a hot climate. Du Tertre (2.475), however, describes European women's dress in the Caribbean thus: 'les femmes des Officiers . . . sont toutes vestuës de des-habillés de tafetas, ou de satin de couleur. De là vient que les rubans sont l'une des bonnes marchandises, & qui a le plus de debit dans le pays, à cause de la prodigieuse quantité qu'il en faut: & j'en ay veu avec d'aussi beaux points de gennes qu'en France' (officers' wives are all dressed in taffeta or coloured satin. Hence ribbons are one of the most sought-after goods with a great turnover, owing to the massive demand for them; and I've seen them wearing as much lace as people in France).

111. *feathers on my head*: For all the contrast Behn is making, it seems that both European and Native American are adorned with feathers. Short hair was unusual for women in the Restoration and may be a concession to the climate or indicate past illness since hair was thought to sap strength.

112. *stuff*: Woven woollen material.

113. *tepeeme*: Cf. Biet (pp. 396 and 412): when the Galibi 'wish to represent a very big number, beyond their ability to count, they show the hairs of their head, saying this word tapoüimé', and 'women speak often' becomes '*oüali orana tapoüimé*'. Warren (p. 26) claims that the Indians express numbers above twenty by crying 'Ounsa awara that is, like the hair of one's Head, innumerable'. And according to Charles de Rochefort, 'When they would signifie a great Number, which goes beyond their Arithmetick, they have no other way than to shew the hair of their Heads, or the sand of the Sea; or they repeat several times the word Mouche, which signifies Much' (*The History of the Caribby-Islands*, trans. John Davies of Kidwelly (1666), p. 73).

114. *Amora tiguamy*: Biet (pp. 395–7) recorded that a familiar Galibi form was *acne tigami* and the second person pronoun *amore*, so that Behn is reporting a greeting.

115. *sarumbo leaf . . . table-cloth*: Biet (p. 416) gives *chalombo* as the name of leaves of trees, which he notes are used as 'serviettes'. Cf. Warren (p. 24): 'their napery is the leaves of the trees'.

116. *mess*: Portion of a meal.

117. *notions or fictions . . . never before seen*: The use of European technology to impress natives of other lands was a feature of many cross-cultural encounters. Captain John Smith had demonstrated a compass and pistol to the North Americans, and Columbus had astonished the Caribs by predicting a lunar eclipse.

118. *peeie*: Biet (pp. 385–8) describes the *piaye* as a doctor; Warren (pp. 26–7) saw the *Peeie* as an impostor and devil-worshipper as well as a healer, and noted that the *Peeie* who does not cure a patient is killed. Ogilby (p. 617) wrote: 'Their Priests, call'd *Peeiaos*, are in great esteem amongst them, because they pretend that they converse with the Spirits *Wattipa* and *Yarakin*, which the *Guianians* exceedingly fear, apprehending themselves often beaten black and blue by them. The *Peeiaos* also profess themselves to be Chirurgeons and Doctors, but if they cure not their Patients, they go in Danger of their Lives, unless they speedily get away.'

119. *several other*: The first edition reverses these two words.

120. *comitias*: Biet (p. 353) claimed that the Indians wore only a piece of clothing called *un camison*. Although he notes the Spanish origin of some Galibi words, he does not connect this with the Spanish *camisa*, used in the region for all kinds of clothing.

121. *contemptibly*: With contempt.

122. *When he . . . died in this debate*: Biet (pp. 376–80), Warren (p. 24) and other travellers describe horrific initiation rites, but Behn seems to have invented this ritual of self-mutilation. It becomes ironic that Oroonoko himself enacts it in the end.

123. *heartburnings*: Resentment.

124. *string . . . knots on it*: Another reference to the numerical systems of the Native Americans. The Incas in particular developed the knotted string into a sophisticated system of calculation used for censuses and book-keeping. Cords of wool or cotton, with other cords suspended from them, were knotted in such a way that amounts were indicated by multiple long knots and spaces between knots (see Thomas Crump, *The Anthropology of Numbers* (Cambridge: Cambridge University Press, 1990), p. 42).

125. *moons*: Months.

126. *gold dust*: There had been stories of a 'golden city' on the Amazon since the previous century; Columbus noted it but did not try to find it and Sir Walter Ralegh made two unsuccessful expeditions in search of it. His *Discovery of Guiana* (1596) includes a description of 'Eldorado' and describes the plainlands as a natural Eden.

In *Paradise Lost* (published the year that Surinam, or Guiana, was ceded to the Dutch), Milton makes a topical reference to 'Guiana, whose great city Geryon's sons / Call El Dorado . . .' (XI.410–11). See also Warren's 'To the Reader': 'In this Continent, the Indians will tell you of Mighty Princes upwards, and Golden Cities, how true I know not.'

127. *River of Amazons*: The mouth of the Amazon is in Brazil and far from Surinam. In seventeenth-century maps it formed the south-eastern border of 'Guiana'. The comparison with the English Thames is especially comic.

128. *guard . . . gold*: In romance guards were always placed on the golden river – something must stand between the adventurer and the realization of the vision.

129. *governor . . . hurricane*: Throughout the period of his ownership, Willoughby attempted to defend the colonies against attack from the Dutch and French and to extend British dominion. During the Second Dutch War, he led an expedition from Barbados to St Christopher (present-day St Kitts) to punish the French for cruelties to the English settlers on the island. On 4 August 1666 he was lost at sea during a storm off the coast of Guadeloupe (see Sir Robert H. Schomburgk, *The History of Barbados* (1848), pp. 290–91). Du Tertre (4.98) claimed that when the people of Guadeloupe heard of Willoughby's design, they had run along the shore imploring the Almighty to send a hurricane to destroy the English squadron: 'l'on voyoit tout le long de la rive, les hommes, & les femmes levans les mains au Ciel, & faisants cette priere avec tant d'instance, qu'il ya quelque apparence qu'ils furent exaucez.'

130. *losing . . . America*: The year 1666–7 was disastrous for English colonization in the Caribbean. After Willoughby's death, the French invaded and ravaged the English settlements on Antigua and Montserrat, burning the sugar works and collecting about a thousand slaves. Only Nevis remained uncaptured. The English counterattacked in 1667, but the French beat off their efforts to recapture St Christopher. Meanwhile Surinam was ceded to the Dutch. 'In little more than a year of combat the English had suffered the most humiliating series of defeats they ever experienced in the West Indies': Richard S. Dunn, *Sugar and Slaves. The Rise of the Planter Class in the English West Indies 1624–1813* (Chapel Hill: University of North Carolina Press, 1972), p. 124.

131. *trades and slaves for four years*: Tradesmen and European slaves

or labourers were indentured for four years through debt, crime or poverty. They could be bought and sold during their time of servitude.

132. *do execution with spirits*: Fight with courage.

133. *county*: Region.

134. *whip and bell*: Method by which dogs were taught obedience, through beatings and discipline.

135. *black Friday*: A day set aside for punishment.

136. *runagades*: Renegades and deserters.

137. *And why ... lash from such hands*: Among the authors Behn might have read, Tryon provides the clearest case against the enslavement of the Africans. Southerne gives Oroonoko blank verse on heroic occasions such as this and differentiates him more sharply than Behn does from the other Africans.

138. *Hannibal ... rocks*: According to Plutarch, when crossing the Alps to make an attack on Rome, 'in certaine places of the highest rockes, [Hannibal] was driven to make passage through, by force of fire and vinegar' (*Lives of the Noble Grecians and Romans*, North's translation, 1579). In the event, Hannibal failed to take Rome; so this became one of the many allusions to failing heroes in the text.

139. *hamaca*: Hammock, from the Carib word, through Spanish *hamaca*; in his *Diary* (21 February 1665: 6.40) Pepys mentions buying 'hammacos' for the navy.

140. *Parhamites ... Parham Plantation*: Supporters of Lord Willoughby in the faction-ridden colony.

141. *ill used and baffled with*: Abused and deceived.

142. *deputy governor*: William Byam, deputy governor of Surinam under the absent Lord Willoughby, and earlier elected leader of the settlers' assembly, became the villain of *Oroonoko*. Behn portrayed him as cowardly, treacherous and dishonourable; yet the critical Henry Adis in *A Letter Sent from Syrranam* (London, 1664) praised 'that worthy person, whom your Lordship hath lately honoured with the Title and Power of your Lieutenant General of this Continent of Guinah'. Biet (pp. 263, 279) also regarded Byam as a brave gentleman of courage and honour, with a most beautiful and sympathetic wife – indeed the Byams were the only civilized couple he encountered in the anarchic colony. He makes no mention of the Indian mistress Behn gives Byam. But Byam may also have been harsh since in 1662 he was accused of cruelty and arbitrariness by a group led by Robert Sanford. He himself wrote two works answering the attacks and complaining

of the insubordinate and unruly ways of the colonists. In *Antigua and the Antiguans. A Full Account of the Colony and its Inhabitants* (1844), p. 318, Mrs Flannigan noted that after the Dutch takeover Byam went with many colonists to Antigua where he held property and became governor. He died there *c.* 1670.

143. *Cat with nine tails*: Whip with nine knotted lashes used in the British navy and army.

144. *basket-hilts*: Swords with rounded protective hilts.

145. *Negroes ... yield*: There are many accounts of slaves committing suicide in desperate circumstances. See Warren (p. 19), and Ligon's *True and Exact History of the Island of Barbados*, pp. 50–51.

146. *abounded his own wit*: Was secure in his own opinion.

147. *composition*: Agreement, compromise.

148. *Christian gods ... honest*: In fact, unlike several other colonizing powers, the English did not press Christianity on the Africans, an omission that Biet (p. 292) much deplored.

149. *In fine*: To conclude.

150. *Fury*: One of the goddesses sent from hell to avenge wrong and punish crime on earth; hence an avenging or tormenting spirit.

151. *those slaves ... lashes*: Behn was contemptuous of turncoats, especially when they were disloyal to her revered James II, from whom support was slipping away during 1688.

152. *my new comedy*: The posthumous *The Younger Brother, Or, The Amorous Jilt*, Behn's comedy not produced until 1696, despite this piece of promotion (*Works* 7.355–417). It was one of two plays apparently rescued from Behn's literary remains by Charles Gildon. Marten, called captain in the historical records of the Surinam militia, is styled colonel here and in the play. Many commented on the number of titles liberally used in the colonies. In his hostile account of Byam in *Surinam Justice*, Sanford ascribed to Marten the ferocity Behn gave to Bannister: Marten 'offered himself the Hangman of any at the Governours single command'.

153. *chirurgeon*: Surgeon.

154. *Newgate*: London prison from which many convicts were exported to work on New World plantations; for example, in 1681 Christopher Jeaffreson bought three hundred convicts from the chief gaoler of Newgate to use on his plantation in Jamaica. See also Behn's *The Widdow Ranter* (*Works* 7.301).

155. *nemine contradicente*: Unanimously (Latin).

156. *Whitehall*: The Palace of Whitehall was built by Cardinal Wolsey;

it had been the principal residence of the sovereign since the time of Henry VIII. It was mainly destroyed by fire in 1697. Willoughby's Parham was under the jurisdiction of Willoughby, the representative of the king, and so, like Whitehall, was above any local law.

157. *we*: The first edition reads 'they'.

158. *mobile*: The mob, rabble (Latin).

159. *sensible*: Sensitive.

160. *fatal stroke*: Oroonoko's killing of Imoinda reinforces the already strong parallel between Oroonoko and the earlier black hero, Shakespeare's Othello.

161. *A bold English ... feet*: In the first edition these two sentences are run on with no punctuation.

162. *ghashly*: Ghastly.

163. *sickly ... melancholy*: Together with the reference to the cropped hair, this suggests that the narrator and possibly Behn herself suffered some illness in Surinam or on the voyage.

164. *Banister*: Major James Bannister negotiated with the Dutch on behalf of the remaining English settlers after the ceding of Surinam. In March 1671 he led about a hundred families to Jamaica where he joined forces with the governor Sir Thomas Lynch who was trying to suppress a rival, backed by other ex-Surinam settlers. Lynch appointed Bannister major-general and let him reorganize the Jamaica militia (see Stephen Saunders Webb, *The Governors-General. The English Army and the Definition of the Empire, 1569–1681* (Chapel Hill: University of North Carolina Press, 1979), p. 228). Jamaica continued boisterous and in 1673 Bannister was murdered by the surveyor general Mr Burford, who was hanged for the crime (see 'A Journal Kept by Col William Beeston From His First Coming to Jamaica', in *Interesting Tracts Relating to the Island of Jamaica* (1800), p. 290). Bannister's characterization as a 'wild Irishman' would remind readers that the Irish labourers taken to the colonies had been the most troublesome. There had been a major rebellion of Irish servants in Barbados in 1647.

165. *post ... tied to it*: Cf. the ending of Macbeth in Shakespeare's tragedy: 'They have tied me to a stake, I cannot flye / But Beare-like I must fight the course' (V.vii.1–2).

166. *tobacco ... pipe*: There are many descriptions of slave-owners giving tobacco to slaves to calm them. See John Stedman, *Narrative of a Five Years' Expedition Against the Revolted Negroes of Surinam* (1796), for a later description of a tortured man smoking

a pipe of tobacco. Stephanie Athey and Daniel Cooper Alarcón in their article '*Oroonoko's* Gendered Economies of Honor/Horror: Reframing Colonial Discourse', *American Literature*, 65 (1993), 415–43, point out that since 'orinoco' also designated a type of tobacco, the 'arresting image of Oroonoko taking tobacco while his own body burns makes literal the analogy between enslaved slave-trader and the commodity for which he is named', thereby signifying 'a transatlantic conjunction of consumer, producer, and commodity' and, more profoundly, representing 'the human beings who are themselves consumed by slavery'.

167. *gave up the ghost*: Died. The phrase is used very frequently in the Authorized Version of the Bible, both in the Old and New Testaments; for example, in Genesis 25:8 Abraham 'gave up the ghost' and in Mark 15:37 and 39 Christ did likewise.

168. *Executioner . . . reproach*: The description of Oroonoko's mutilation and death has some similarities with the account of the death of John Allin, the failed European assassin of Willoughby. The account, with mention of the barbecuing and mutilation of Allin, as well as his Roman-inspired heroism, is given by Byam in *An Exact Relation of the Most Execrable Attempts of John Allin, Committed on the Person of His Excellency Francis Lord Willoughby of Parham, Captain General of the Continent of Guiana & of all the Carriby Islands, and our Lord Protector* (1665). Byam ends rather like Behn in *Oroonoko*: 'Thus dies this atheist.' Both the deaths of Allin and Oroonoko have similarities with that of Plutarch's Julius Caesar, who is met with blows on all sides and hedged round like a wild beast. Biet (p. 291) gives harrowing descriptions of contemporary slave punishment: 'The overseer, after having had him [the slave] treated so [beaten by his fellow-slaves] for seven or eight days, cut off one of his ears, caused it to be roasted, and made him eat it.' Du Tertre (2.532) notes the need for harsh punishment in all the European colonies using slave-labour: 'Les Négres fugitifs, & particulierement ceux qui débauchent les autres, sont chastiez fort rigoureusement; car on les attache à un Pilier, & apres qu'on leur a découpé toute la peau à coups de Liannes, on frotte leurs playes avec du Piment, du Sel, & de jus de Citron, ce qui leur cause des douleurs incroyables' (Escaped Negroes, especially ringleaders, meet with very cruel punishment; they are tied to a post, whipped until their skin is cut all over, and then they rub their wounds with pepper, salt and lemon juice, which causes them indescribable pain). The physician and naturalist, later secretary to the Royal Society, Hans Sloane,

in his *Voyage to the Islands Madera, Barbados, Nieves, S. Chris-tophers and Jamaica, with the Natural History of the Herbs and Trees, Four-footed Beasts, Fishes, Birds, Insects, Reptiles, &c.* (1707), 1.lvii, also notes the cruel punishments for 'Rebellions' in which the slaves are punished by 'nailing them down on the ground with crooked Sticks on every Limb, and then applying the Fire by degrees from the Feet and Hands, burning them gradually up to the Head, whereby their pains are extravagant'.

THE STORY OF PENGUIN CLASSICS

Before 1946 ...'Classics' are mainly the domain of academics and students, without readable editions for everyone else. This all changes when a little-known classicist, E. V. Rieu, presents Penguin founder Allen Lane with the translation of Homer's *Odyssey* that he has been working on and reading to his wife Nelly in his spare time.

1946 *The Odyssey* becomes the first Penguin Classic published, and promptly sells three million copies. Suddenly, classic books are no longer for the privileged few.

1950s Rieu, now series editor, turns to professional writers for the best modern, readable translations, including Dorothy L. Sayers's *Inferno* and Robert Graves's *The Twelve Caesars*, which revives the salacious original.

1960s The Classics are given the distinctive black jackets that have remained a constant throughout the series's various looks. Rieu retires in 1964, hailing the Penguin Classics list as 'the greatest educative force of the 20th century'.

1970s A new generation of translators arrives to swell the Penguin Classics ranks, and the list grows to encompass more philosophy, religion, science, history and politics.

1980s The Penguin American Library joins the Classics stable, with titles such as *The Last of the Mohicans* safeguarded. Penguin Classics now offers the most comprehensive library of world literature available.

1990s The launch of Penguin Audiobooks brings the classics to a listening audience for the first time, and in 1999 the launch of the Penguin Classics website takes them online to a larger global readership than ever before.

The 21st Century Penguin Classics are rejacketed for the first time in nearly twenty years. This world famous series now consists of more than 1300 titles, making the widest range of the best books ever written available to millions – and constantly redefining the meaning of what makes a 'classic'.

The Odyssey continues ...

The best books ever written

PENGUIN CLASSICS

SINCE 1946

Find out more at www.penguinclassics.com